CLINICALLY DEAD

A DR CATHY MORELAND MYSTERY #BOOK FIVE

MAIRI CHONG

BLOODHOUND
— BOOKS —

www.bloodhoundbooks.com

Print ISBN 978-1-914614-92-7

ALSO BY MAIRI CHONG

For W – never prouder

1

'Is that you? What a fright you gave me!'

She opened the door wider and peered into the night. It took a moment or two for her eyes to adjust to the dark, but when she could focus, she tutted. The man outside was slumped partially against the door frame. He made a snorting sound.

'How drunk are you?'

She fumbled for the light switch, all the while talking loudly. 'Gave me a hell of a fright when I saw the shadow at the window. And you'd not answered your phone either. How much did you have this time then? You stink to high heaven of it. You've not been sick, have you? I can smell it from here. Half the neighbours will have heard you thumping about too.'

The man did not answer, but swayed and then slowly buckled. He slid to his knees, his breath escaping in a moan.

'Oh, for goodness' sake,' she scolded. 'We're too old for this nonsense. You'll be sorry in the morning. Come on.'

She took her husband's jacket sleeve and tugged. Her hand touched something warm and damp, and she recoiled. 'You've thrown up all down yourself. In the name of God!'

By the hall light, she looked at her hand. Her skin was pale and her fingers trembled. *Blood.*

'How many times have you been sick? You've vomited your guts up, you idiot.'

She crouched down, slotting an arm under his own and half dragged, half carried him into the house. The door was still open, but the stench of alcohol and vomit made her gag.

She cursed, but stopped. His face was an odd pallor and his eyes rolling.

'You're in a mess.' She knew she was talking too loudly. Her voice seemed to echo into the darkness outside.

She bent down and felt his forehead. Cold and clammy.

His skin had a yellowish-grey hue and, as he lay on the floor at her feet, he drew his knees up to his chest.

'You're not right. This isn't right. What have you taken?' she demanded. 'Oh, God! I'm frightened. Open your eyes, for goodness' sake! Not that stuff again.'

He seemed to make an almighty effort, but his teeth were clenched in a painful snarl.

She ran to the open doorway and looked wildly up and down the street. The light in their neighbours' downstairs front room was still on. Whimpering to herself, she told him not to move, but she was in such a panic now that she couldn't decide what to do for the best and found herself frozen. What would someone do in these circumstances? She shouldn't leave him. Perhaps she should boil the kettle. Make a hot coffee.

'Hello? Everything all right out there?' A man's voice suddenly came.

She peered out into the darkness.

'Oh God, no,' she wailed. 'He's not well. I think something's wrong. It was a work night out. I thought he was drunk but it's worse than that. His face is odd, and he's been sick. There's blood in it.'

The neighbour, a man in his late sixties, came out of the house next door and stood in his dressing gown on the wide stone step looking over the hedge. 'Do you want me to come over? If you're worried, shouldn't you call for help? An ambulance? I thought you were medically trained yourself?'

She tutted and went back inside, slamming the door. He had been quite enough help, thank you. Working in the hospital didn't make her a bloody paramedic. By now, her husband had pressed himself against the skirting board and was arching his back. His head was tilted and his eyes appeared to be unseeing.

'An ambulance,' she said to herself. 'Of course, that's what I need to do.' She stepped over him and into the living room, closing the door behind her. She stood for some moments with her back to the door. In the hallway, she could hear him groaning and shifting. It was all right. If she slowed her breathing, it would be all right.

The phone was on the table. She dived across the room and held it, but her hands were shaking too much. Instead of dialling, she stared at the number nine, almost willing it to call itself. 'Help,' she mouthed at the inanimate object. 'Help me!'

There was a sharp rap at the front door. She shrieked and dropped the phone. It fell to the floor and rolled under the sofa.

'Shit! Oh God, help!' she howled.

Wishing she didn't have to face the horror of the hallway again, she reluctantly opened the living room door and, trying to avert her eyes, stepped over her husband once more. The cold air from outside hit her, making her tremble even more. Her neighbour stood on the step, peering in.

'Something very wrong there,' he said, studying the man, who was now barely conscious on the carpet.

When she could bring herself to do so she looked also and saw that he had been sick once again. Beside his mouth was a small pool of frothy, pinkish fluid.

'That's not booze,' the neighbour pronounced, shaking his head. 'Have you called yet?'

'Called?'

'The ambulance?'

'I– I was just... I wondered about a hot coffee. I didn't want to waste anyone's time, but now...'

The neighbour shook his head. 'Looks serious. A hospital job, I'd say. You'd better call.' He crouched down and looked at the man. 'All right, mate? Maybe had a bit of a fit? I had a cousin with epilepsy. Would he have taken something he shouldn't, do you think?'

'No! What the hell are you suggesting? No, of course not. He's not some drug addict if that's what you mean! Listen, we're fine. I'm fine. If you just leave us, I've got things in order.'

The elderly neighbour straightened up, still shaking his head. 'He's trying to say something, look.'

They both gazed down. The man's breathing was shallow. It came in shuddering gasps. He looked up at them. First at the nosy neighbour and then to his wife. He reached out a hand. 'H– H– H–' he said, but the effort was too great.

'Yes?' his wife said in desperation. 'H– what? What are you trying to say? What should we do? Is it hospital? Have you swallowed something? Something accidentally? What is it?'

They waited.

'H–'

His eyes widened with what appeared to be another spasm of pain, and then, with his gaze still fixed on his wife, he died.

2

No one would have thought from Sara's expression as she worked at the computer, that her mind was simmering with unrequited passion. Unfortunately, for everyone concerned, it was not for her husband. When had it begun? It had been gradual, she decided. Yes. The feeling had crept up on her. It was absurd, of course. She had seen his wife in the corridor several times. He spoke of her often, as it happened. Over coffee break yesterday, he had dropped her into the conversation. Sara grimaced. The lovely Victoria. Going away for the weekend with some of her girlfriends from nursing college. Sara imagined her, all snooty and arrogantly beautiful, kissing Michael on the cheek. Her lips red, and a silk scarf knotted at her neck. Silly. People didn't even wear silk scarves these days, but it was how she imagined her. Sara thought of Michael alone in the house that weekend.

She shook her head in self-disgust. Absurd. A senseless crush, and at her age, too. She had two grown-up daughters of her own, and Michael was old enough to be her son. She returned to her dictation and tried to put the thought from her mind.

Working in the pathology office had not been her first choice. She'd have preferred a quiet GP surgery. But she'd been lucky to get the job at all. Medical secretaries were ten-a-penny, and she was in her late forties. Employers liked flashy young girls who understood the intricacies of computers. But there was a good deal to be said for experience, and she had plenty of that. The job was pretty straightforward and at least you didn't have doctors waltzing in and out making demands all the time. These pathology medics were a different class from the general practitioners altogether. Suave and intelligent.

Before she had started working there eighteen months ago, she had conjured up all kinds of gruesome images of dead bodies lying about, of forensic scientists standing in white coats, scalpels in hand. But it wasn't like that at all. Most of the work they did was assessing tissues sent up to the labs by the surgeons or the local doctors' surgeries. Sara had to type up the reports dictated by the pathology doctors, of which there were three: Dr Bhat, Professor Huxley and Michael. She enjoyed the work on the whole. Agnes, who worked beside her, was a bit of a bore, of course, but she was nearing retirement. The lab assistants could lord it up from time to time too. But all the downsides paled into insignificance...

Michael. Things had changed when he joined the team three months ago. She'd seen several registrar doctors come and go as part of their hospital rotation. Michael was different, though. Pathology, he said, was going to be his final resting place. They'd had a giggle about his turn of phrase when he said it, especially given that they did indeed perform all the hospital post-mortems. Nothing exciting, of course. Sara had had to type up most of the reports. The majority of people died of very dull things indeed. Pneumonia, myocardial infarctions, pulmonary emboli. Nothing juicy at all. Anything with a whiff of suspicion went to the police mortuary. It was a pity in many ways. But if

Michael intended to stay put long term, it would certainly make her days more entertaining.

All morning, Sara diligently listened to her dictation with Agnes working at the desk across the room. Michael was busy in the labs, but he passed the office once and paused at the window, grinning in at her. A curl of dark brown hair had fallen across his forehead. He had a fine forehead; wide and clear. His eyes too... Sara felt her face flush. She smiled and lifted a hand to wave, but he was gone. She glanced across at Agnes, who raised an eyebrow.

'What?'

Agnes removed her glasses. 'I didn't say anything, Sara.' The older secretary looked at her in a weary sort of a way and sighed. 'You know what they're like, these medics? He's playing you a fine game, that one.'

Sara snorted. 'Don't be ridiculous. We're just friends. He's nearly twenty years younger than me anyway and we're both married.'

Agnes nodded sagely and returned to her dictation.

Interfering old bat, Sara thought, and they worked in silence until lunchtime.

The department had begun a bit of a tradition of having lunch together. Sara wasn't sure who had instigated it. One of the lab technicians, probably. All the doctors came along. Sara found herself walking in step with Michael as they arrived at the canteen that day. She would be sure to choose something light to eat. A salad sandwich, perhaps. Nothing messy. She recalled the first meal out with her husband, John, over twenty years ago, now. He had taken her to a curry house on the high street and, after a lovely meal, he had walked her home, only then telling her she had a sliver of spinach stuck to her front tooth. Aloo something or other, it had been. She'd never eaten it again.

In the canteen, they settled at their usual table at the far end.

Other departments seemed to do the same, but the pathology labs were the largest group, so they needed to pull two tables together and shift some chairs. Dr Bhat, one of the consultants, ensured that everyone had a seat. He and Professor Huxley, despite being the most senior in the medical team, were quite gentlemanly.

Agnes had brought a packed lunch, as she always did, and, annoyingly, settled herself next to Sara. The chair on the other side was still free, though. Jennifer, Ettie and Hughie, the lab technicians, sat opposite. They had been having some difficulties with the chemicals. Hughie was saying something to Professor Huxley about the suppliers being less than reliable and that the stuff they had ordered differed from usual.

'Maybe they don't take the complaint seriously when it comes from a lowly lab technician,' Hughie was saying. 'Surely, being in the hospital counts for something. I had to deal with the most dreadful cheek from some silly young girl on the phone and even then, she said I'd need to call back.'

'I'll look into it this afternoon,' Dr Bhat promised.

Professor Huxley scowled. 'You've enough on already, Saj. I'll get Michael to see to it. He's done next-to-nothing all morning anyway, and as for the research project, he's been more of a hindrance than a help.'

Sara looked across the busy canteen. Michael appeared to be having some difficulty with the toasted sandwich he had ordered. The woman behind the counter seemed to have made up his order wrong, and he stood propped against the hot metal ledge, chatting to people as they passed with their lunch trays. He looked across at their table now. Agnes nudged Sara in the ribs, making her jump.

'Staring,' the older woman mouthed.

Sara took a bite from her sandwich, far more savagely than she had intended.

'All well, ladies?' Dr Bhat asked them, perhaps noticing the tension at their side of the table. 'I know it's been busy in the office today. Are we on top of things? No problems at all?'

'None,' Agnes said. 'Sara's having a bit of a mid-life crisis, that's all that's wrong here.'

Sara glared at her colleague.

'Oh, I can't believe you'd describe Sara as mid-life,' Michael said, now standing at the table with his tray. It seemed that he had finally received the correct order. 'Surely, she's barely even in her thirties.' He showed an irregular flash of teeth. So white. Sara would replay the embarrassment and enjoyment over and over in her mind for days to come. 'What have you got to have a crisis about anyway, Sara? I hope your husband's behaving.'

Sara snorted and was repulsed by herself. 'Nothing changes with John. Spends half his life either under a car or on his beloved building site.'

Michael settled himself in the chair beside her and began dissecting his toasted sandwich with the precision of a surgeon. Slim, tapering fingers, Sara thought as she watched his hands on the cutlery, and blushed again. Oh God, she really must get a grip.

'Michael?' Prof Huxley said from the other end of the table. 'We were just talking. Hughie mentioned that the suppliers have muddled up the chemicals that they sent. Can you look at what we have this afternoon? He's already tried to speak to someone about it and they're being rather awkward.'

Michael grinned. 'Sure. I'm sick of pap smears, anyway.' He leaned in towards Sara. 'If I have to look at another bloody cervical sample, I'll go mad. I've got a stinker of a hangover as well. I know I'm a lowly registrar, but really, was this what I trained for?'

Sara tutted and smirked. 'You're doing an important job.'

'Oh sure. I know. If the techies weren't so insecure about their decisions though, I'd not have to do half of it.'

Sara looked up and saw Hughie frown. He had been in the department for a good deal longer than Michael, and was undoubtedly experienced at his job. Generally, he and the two female lab technicians did indeed see to the simple cytology. This was part of their remit, along with preparing the slides and equipment for the doctors. It was only if they had a borderline sample that they asked the doctors to look. Michael was only a registrar, so this task fell to him.

Sara continued to eat her sandwich carefully.

'Not on the ball, though,' Michael continued, still speaking in a playful voice and looking across at Hughie. 'Not on the ball. I wonder why though...'

Everyone else was chatting and seemed not to notice. Sara looked at Hughie. It was only there for a second before he turned to Ettie and Jennifer and began to talk. It was hard to describe, but as she slowly chewed, she considered Hughie's expression. Yes, it was odd. His eyes had been quite strange. Michael had only been teasing, too. People were funny, though. They had insecurities you didn't even know about.

Sara recalled something her mother had said to her once when, as a girl when she fell out with a friend at school. 'Everyone has something going on,' her mother had said. 'You never know what happens behind closed doors, or what people are thinking.' Looking across the table again at Hughie, Sara wondered.

3

Sara was too preoccupied to think about the spat between Hughie and Michael again for a few days. She was busy in the office because neurosurgery was doing several cancer resections in theatre and needed the pathologists ready to report on any samples immediately so that they could continue or abandon the treatment on the operating table. Sara had had to phone through to the secretaries half a dozen times with updates. It was quite exhausting and stressful too, knowing that a surgeon was waiting for her call.

She'd had a good deal on her mind recently anyway, what with her mum. Perhaps work wasn't her main focus. They'd kept on top of things for a while, but it wasn't great. Her mother lived next door, well, at the bottom of their garden, actually, in a granny flat. The arrangement had worked for the past five years, but even Sara could see that it couldn't go on forever.

That morning, the smell had hit her as soon as she walked in. When she called out, there was no answer. Not that she had expected one. She fumbled along the wall, her fingers tracing the pimples, feeling them like hives on the membrane of the house. Why they had chosen woodchip wallpaper was beyond her. It was already out of fashion. When she found the light switch, the passageway was ablaze. She blinked and instinctively focused on the carpet to avoid the glare. But the sight that met her was far from pleasant. On the brown geometric pattern was a towel. It had been laid out almost as if its user had deliberately done so. One corner was outstretched, rakishly leading the visitor towards the door of the living room. The towel was once white. Now it was not.

'Mum? Where are you?'

Still no answer. She bypassed the beckoning towel and then a trail of unthinkable mess. The incontinence pads were strewn in a blue and white crazy-paving across the floor. Her mother had found not only a toilet roll but the kitchen roll also. Both had been unravelled and scattered at random. All absorbent items, Sara credited her mother with that, but none used with suitable care or understanding. How she would clean the carpet later, she didn't know.

Her mother had found her way back to the bedroom and was perched on the edge of the bed in semi-darkness. She was unrecognisable. Where once had sat a broad-shouldered woman with unusually strong features and razor-sharp wit, now huddled a fragile, old lady. Sara wanted to avert her gaze from the bare sagging flesh, but found herself transfixed.

She was reminded of the first time she had walked into the pathology labs at work to pass on a message to one of the doctors. The main labs were for simple microscopic work. Further inside, though, past two sets of heavy doors were the actual hospital post-mortem rooms. Sara had not been that far into the building before, but seeing that Professor Huxley must only be there, she had ventured through the door marked: 'Private.' Sara shook her head ruefully at the memory. She was used to it now, of course, but seeing a dead body for the first time... well, it had made her jittery. Then also, she had found her eyes wandering over the room and fixing on the prone form. The professor must have realised. He had called out to ask what he could do to help. She had answered. Her voice was stammering. Her unsteady words had echoed all around the room. All the while, her eyes were fixed on the pale, mottled remains that had once been someone's father, brother or husband. She felt much the same about her mother now. It was like looking at a dead person. A vacant shell. Sara never knew how vast the emptiness inside her mother would become, or how loud the echoes would reverberate, until the disease took hold.

There was a lump in her throat. Sara swallowed.

'Mum, you're in a pickle again.'

The woman, who was once her mother, agreed that perhaps she was.

It took an hour and a half to get her sorted. She was quite cold. Sara quickly decided that the only option was the shower. Her mother hated this at the best of times, but she couldn't get the mess off of her legs without running water. Recently, the old woman had taken an irrational dislike to the bathroom, and for the past few weeks, they had been compromising with hot flannels and soap. Not that morning, though.

Her mother had never suffered fools gladly, and that day, Sara knew she must find her completely intolerable. She tried to switch off from the words. They were nonsensical. Filled with repetition. Sometimes her mother got stuck in a loop.

'Ba, ba, ba, ba, ba, ba...' Until finally, it came: 'Bitch-cow!'

It was a relief when she got it out. The anticipation was almost worse. She had never spoken like that before. Not ever.

Sara gulped back hysterical laughter as she tussled the soiled nightdress over her mother's head, trying to be as gentle as she could, despite the other woman deliberately trying to replace it at the same time. She wondered how the garment had transformed from soft, fleecy cotton to this inelastic straightjacket. Sara murmured encouragement, slowly explaining what she was doing and why, coaxing with promises of warm soapy water and fresh towels. This talk was for herself, of course. Sara heard her voice as a listener might an audiobook. The spoken word rhythmic and gentle. If she thought about what she was doing, she might go insane. Her dialogue continued from bed to bathroom and back again. She shut off from seeing anything, going through the motions like an automaton. Perhaps she was the empty shell and not her mother after all. Sometimes she felt completely hollow.

After the shower blasphemy was forgotten and her mother was in bed, the old lady smiled. Her hair was a halo of feathery white and her cheeks tinged with pink, like glowing rose petals.

'What time do you finish, dear?'

I never finish, Mum, I'm your bloody daughter, Sara wanted to say, but instead, she told her she clocked off soon.

Her mother beamed indulgently and Sara wished for the hundredth time that returning from work that evening, she would find her mother still smiling gently, but cold to the touch.

'Put a pillow over my face,' she had once whispered. 'Put me out of my misery. Go on. No one needs to know.'

Sara had laughed at the time and told her not to be a dafty. She'd get her arrested if anyone heard talk like that. She had tried to brush it off as a senseless moment, but, if she was completely honest, it was probably during one of her mother's more lucid flashes. And she had said those awful words with her heart, holding on to Sara's arm until the skin pinched and hurt. Sara had told no one about it. Not even John. She wondered what Michael would have said. She'd mentioned her mother to him during a coffee break, explaining how hard things were. He had been sympathetic, so understanding. It made her wonder why he had chosen to become a pathology doctor, with his only patients being dead ones. Michael was better than that. He could change someone's day with a look, just a smile. Did he know how important he was? Certainly, had it not been for his presence in her life, she might well have gone off the rails. Why he and Hughie had locked horns was a mystery. She recalled the odd exchange over lunch only days before and wondered what it had been about. Hughie blew hot and cold all the time, though. When the labs were under pressure to get samples through, he was a nightmare.

Yesterday, she'd been speaking to the lab technicians about the chemical suppliers. The stuff that had been ordered was all wrong, and Michael had checked it and said it would have to go back.

'Would you like me to see to it? It'll be by special courier, I suppose? I've never had to send anything back before,' she had offered.

'It's up to the techies,' Michael said, as he walked past. 'You shouldn't be going anywhere near it.'

Sara had looked up to see concern written on his face. She had enough on her plate with her dictations, but she'd do it happily for him. 'I don't mind. Leave it with me,' she promised.

Michael smiled. A slow smile, the kind that crept at the corners of the mouth and then transformed the entire face. 'You're a star,' he said. 'This place would be lost without you.'

Out of interest, she had asked Hughie and Jennifer why the chemical was so hazardous, anyway.

'Poison,' Hughie stated. 'Nasty stuff. Kill you in a matter of minutes. Only a small amount. It's the wrong stuff for us though and no use. I'll package it up later. Make sure it's ready to go back if you're dealing with it now. We're busy enough as it is, without this.'

Sara nodded, all the while thinking of her poor mother. If she knew it would be quick, she might have been tempted...

4

D r Cathy Moreland inclined her head. These conversations were difficult but sometimes allowing the relative to lead the discussion worked out for the best in the end.

Before her, Mrs Sara Wiseman was seated, her legs crossed and folded behind her in the consulting room chair. Her hands were clasped tightly so that the knuckles showed white.

'No, it's not such a surprise,' Mrs Wiseman said and bit her lip.

Cathy waited.

'I mean, I've not spoken with John...' The other woman looked skywards and Cathy wondered if she was blinking back tears, but when she met her gaze once more, the focus did not waver. 'I'll agree, of course. I'd be glad to. John's hardly involved and she's my mother.'

Cathy smiled slightly, her grey eyes full of compassion. She'd had this conversation with families multiple times before when a relative neared their end of life. Sometimes it was straightforward. With terminal cancer, she often had a frank conversation with the patient and they agreed together about their end-of-life care. With Alzheimer's disease, things could be more difficult. The decline in health was gradual, the steps towards the end were often staggered and of different heights. It was a big ask of the family, making that decision, but as Cathy phrased it, they had to think of those last hours and if Sara Wiseman's failing mother did have a collapse of some sort, things would need to be in place. Decisions would have to be made. As it was, if Sara found her mother unresponsive, she'd be duty-bound to call an ambulance crew who would then have to perform CPR. It was highly questionable now if that was the right thing for the old lady. Her only daughter had power of attorney, and so the decision fell to her.

Sara nodded, perhaps to force the point. 'No. If anything happened, I wouldn't want that. No heroics. No chest compressions and that sort of thing. She's past that. She's too old and frail. What would be the point? No, what you say is really what I've been thinking myself. If there was an easier way, I wish I knew it. I suppose we just watch her go downhill, do we? Do you have any idea how long?'

Cathy spread her hands wide. 'It's so difficult to say. And I'm not saying we're withholding treatment at all. If she had a urine infection or something minor of that sort, we would make her comfortable with antibiotics, of course. But if she went downhill dramatically with the Alzheimer's... Well, I just felt it right to ask you at this point. I know it's been hard for you to care for her. I wish I could predict. You've told me already that she seems quite lucid but that it's becoming far less regular?'

Mrs Wiseman sighed. 'Awful, at times. She barely knows who I am and yet, sometimes, we do seem to connect. The other day, she mentioned my father. She spoke about him clearly, as if she remembered so well.'

Cathy heard the sadness in her voice. Sara looked tired. Her face was made up, but concealer failed to cover the darkness below her eyes.

'How are you in yourself?'

Sara shifted in her chair, and Cathy felt she had been too direct. But the question had to be asked.

'Fine, fine. I manage. Well, I have to, don't I? No one's going to jump in and do it all for me, are they?' She laughed a little, and her hands fidgeted in her lap. 'John built the granny flat to make it easier. And it does. I just can't switch off. Does that make sense? I'm not complaining. Like I say, I'm fine. I cope.' She laughed again.

'The district nurses have put in the notes that they've suggested respite, even for a few days...'

Mrs Wiseman shook her head. 'Not needed. Thank you. I appreciate the offer. No. If you can sign the form now, I'd be grateful.'

'Obviously, if anything changes...' Cathy said.

'It won't though, will it?' Sara challenged. 'She won't improve. She'll only get worse. I wish we were kinder to ourselves. You wouldn't watch a dog going through this. It'd be put out of its misery, and a good thing too. Cruel. A cruel disease, that's what it is.'

'I'm sorry,' Cathy said.

Sara Wiseman stooped to collect her bag from the floor. 'It's not your fault. It's no one's fault, is it? It's just I have to see it every bloody day. I have to live with it more than my mother.'

5

Sara had to force herself to walk past without staring. She concentrated on the floor in front of her. Don't look left. Don't look left. They were standing in the corridor outside the labs. Michael had his arm up resting on the wall, as if blocking her way and the woman, who Sara had watched from afar and despised, slouched, arms folded, her nurses' uniform fitted and more cinched in at the waist than was surely necessary or comfortable. Her dark hair was immaculately slicked back into a high ponytail, and her make-up was flawless. Sara moved quickly, hoping not to be seen, but she half tripped on the polished linoleum and Michael's attention moved from his beautiful wife to his secretary.

'Sara!' he called out, dropping his arm and moving away from the woman he had chosen, for better or worse. 'I was just saying to Vic that you and I were planning an illicit evening together.'

Sara gaped and knew that she was blushing. 'I– I don't know what you mean.' She looked from Michael, whose mouth twitched into a crooked grin, to Victoria, who didn't smile at all.

'Vic, this is my saviour, Sara. Secretary, but a whole lot more.

About the only person I like in the bloody place. She regularly saves my ass when I'm running late or in a fix, don't you, Sara?'

Sara smiled but felt her stomach churn with awkwardness.

'But haven't you heard yet?' Michael teased. 'Our work night out. Surely Ettie or Jennifer mentioned it? It's been the talk of the town all morning. Well, the lab's anyway. The prof's apparently footing the bill, so I'm all for it.'

Sara swallowed. A group of nurses coming along the corridor jostled past, giggling.

'No. No one's said...' she began. She looked at Victoria, but the other woman seemed disinterested and appeared to have seen someone else in the distance.

'I need to go,' Victoria said. 'Nice to meet you, Sara.' She moved as if to touch Michael, but he stepped back.

'Catch you later,' he said and took Sara's arm. 'Back to it, Sara,' he said, and guided her along the corridor.

Sara's heart was in her mouth. Through the fabric of her cotton blouse, she felt his hand warm on her elbow. She wanted him to hold her forever.

It took her an eternity to settle after that, and when Ettie did eventually come in to tell her and Agnes about the planned meal out, she had almost decided that she wasn't going. How could she go? She'd make a dreadful fool of herself once again in front of Michael, and his affection would turn to distaste if he had to sit and speak with her for any length of time.

'Oh, come on, Sara, why not come?' Ettie said.

Sara looked up at the lab technician, who stood in the office in her white coat.

'I'm not sure...' she repeated, but Ettie was shaking her head.

'You know it would do you good. It'd do all of us good. The professor is calling it a bit of a morale boost. We've been snapping at one another these past few weeks. I suppose the old man must have finally noticed and decided to do something about it. I've seen how busy it's been in here for you guys, too. A treat, he's saying. The department foots the bill. Free meal, free booze. Hughie made sure to double-check on that. You know how hard up he always is? He actually said to the prof that the techies wouldn't come otherwise. Said we're paid barely enough to live on!'

Sara raised her eyebrows in surprise.

'Hughie does go on a bit.' Ettie laughed. 'It's embarrassing sometimes the way he says things. God knows it's nothing to do with the old professor what our wages are. Well then, what do you think? Will you come? It would be awkward with just the medics and us techies. It always is over lunch when you don't come down to the canteen and it'll fall to me and Jennifer to keep the chat going.'

Agnes shrugged. 'I've nothing on. But I can't offer much in the way of sparkling conversation to you young things. You said a week on Thursday, didn't you?'

'I've not confirmed with everyone, but yes. That's the plan. The prof asked Hughie to book a table later today if we have enough takers.'

'I'm surprised at *you* hesitating, Sara,' Agnes said meaningfully.

Sara rolled her eyes. She smiled at Ettie. 'Okay, that'll be fine. Put my name down but it'll depend on how Mum is.'

'Excellent. I'll get Hughie onto it later. Any funny food things, by the way? Allergies? Stuff like that?'

'I don't like curry,' Sara quickly said, remembering the spinach.

'Okay. I'll let him know.' Ettie made her way to the door, but with her hand on the handle, she turned back. 'Oh, the courier came then, did they?'

Sara looked up. Her mouth was suddenly dry. 'I– I think...'

'It was just I saw that the fume cupboard was empty this

morning. I assume they picked up the stuff being returned? It should have been one of us seeing to it. Goodness knows how you got roped in. Was it yesterday evening after we all left? I hope you didn't have to stay back late?'

'Yes,' Sara said, and swallowed. 'No, it was fine.'

'Cool. Thanks for that. Okay, I'll leave you to it. Cheers, ladies.'

The door shut. Sara could feel Agnes's eyes on her. She purposefully repositioned the headphones and rested her fingers on the computer keyboard in feigned concentration.

6

In the end, the entire department agreed to the meal. In many ways, the anticipation did indeed seem to bolster morale, and the event was mentioned half a dozen times at coffee and lunch breaks. Sara had told John about it one evening, but only after having let him settle a bit.

He had arrived home later than her and was in a foul temper. She could tell what mood he was in by the way he closed the front door. An abrupt entrance without dialogue and a forceful thump as his boots were kicked aside, indicated a bad day.

There had been an accident on the building site. Reading between the lines, it must have shaken him a bit. John didn't often show his emotions. She could imagine that if he had had a fright, he might well be furious, especially if he'd shown it in front of the others.

It seemed that one of the new lads hadn't put the safety catch or hook onto the crane correctly, and when the next boy came to turn it, the top part came crashing down and clipped him on the shoulder. John had gone with him to the hospital. Sara felt strange imagining John in the same building as her, albeit on a different floor.

'You should have come up,' she said, but she didn't mean it. That would have been dreadful. To have John invading her workplace would have been unimaginable.

He said that he had to sit in A&E with this young lad and wait for over an hour to be seen. Apparently, there had been a road traffic accident brought in, and they could hear the doctors and nurses working on the injured man in the next room. By the time they were seen, John had been in a state. The lad had to have his shoulder put back in because it was dislocated, and he would be off work for at least two months now.

Sara made the expected consoling noises. By the time he had finished his tale and their meal was eaten, she didn't have the heart to tell him about her work night out and instead left it until they were getting ready for bed. If John wasn't in the right frame of mind to hear something, it wasn't worth bothering. She picked her moments more and more these days. It wasn't as if they argued. That required too much effort, and neither of them could commit to it. Somehow, they seemed to glide through life without needing to bother about each other at all.

'I thought you hated half of them,' he replied, turning to look at her when she finally told him.

Sara paused, still folding the cardigan she had taken off. 'Only Agnes gets on my nerves, and I don't hate her. She just irritates me. She's a bit of a bore. An old sourpuss. We hardly speak, despite sitting in the same room every day. When I think about it, I know next-to-nothing about her.'

'What about that fussy professor? I can't believe he's coming along. God knows what he'll have to talk about. Wasn't he nagging about typing errors in his reports at the start? I seem to remember you and him disagreeing over something or other.

Then there was the young girl who was lording it up about something. Took a dislike to you, I thought.'

'Ettie? She's a bit snooty in the office sometimes, yes. She and Hughie seem to think they're better qualified than the doctors sometimes. They've been in the job for a while, of course, and are good at what they do as lab technicians. I suppose when the new doctors start working in the department, it must be a little galling for them, being bossed around by someone who knows less than they do.'

'Well, whatever, but it seems to me like it would be an evening of hell. All of those jumped-up medics and weirdo scientists.'

'We get on. We all do. There's a bit of jockeying for position. But the professor and Dr Bhat smooth things over a good deal. I think it'll be fun. One of the medics is nice. He makes us all laugh.' Sara turned away, unable to look at him.

'God knows how you ended up in the place, anyway. Last thing I'd have expected you to do. Working in a mortuary. It's enough to give you nightmares.'

She rolled her eyes. 'It's not that, and you know it. Listen, I'll just nip down to the kitchen. I've forgotten to make up Mum's breakfast tray and I'll only end up running late in the morning when I go across.'

'And you think she'd notice if you were late?'

Sara sighed and went to the door. She couldn't remember the last time John had understood. How had they grown so far apart? When they first met and married, they had been in love. When the kids had come along this had rapidly changed to amicable companionship. Now that they were alone once more with the children long since flown the nest, what was left?

She looked across at her husband as he stepped out of his jeans. She studied him properly for the first time in many weeks, taking in his pale legs, his T-shirt taut across his belly. She felt a pang of something. Sara swallowed. She knew it wasn't love. Guilt, perhaps? But for what? She couldn't force herself to love him, and what did it matter, anyway? She doubted very much if he felt any affection for her these days. It was probably the same for many couples of their age. People fell out of love but stayed together out of habit. It was too hard to put in the extra effort to pay one another compliments and make little romantic gestures day-in, day-out. Back at the start, John had brought her flowers once a month when he got his pay packet. He had turned on the radiator in the bathroom in the morning to warm her towel. She smiled recalling how smart he had once been and how proud she had felt holding his arm.

As she descended the stairs, she thought of the house they had moved into when they had just married. It was on the other side of town, up on Bridge Street. A home where they had brought up the girls. It had felt different then. Everything had been different on Bridge Street. Why they had moved to this awful cul-de-sac, she didn't know. Of course, the house had been too big by the time the girls had gone. Her mother's health had declined, and so had their marriage.

Oh, she knew he was unhappy, too. She'd seen the pills stuffed down the side of his bedside cabinet in between a book he never read and a handkerchief. God alone knew what they were. Pep-pills, she thought. Or antidepressants of some kind, although they didn't look like prescription things, more like herbal stuff you bought online. She'd waited for him to tell her about them, but he never had.

No, a good deal had changed since they first met. At least she still took pride in her appearance. She'd not let that slip. She'd been walking into work these past few months rather than catching the bus. Already, her calves were looking more toned. Sara would go into town perhaps tomorrow and buy that skirt she'd been wanting. She'd seen it in the posh shop on the corner. Her wages would stretch to it, and she'd need something nice for the night out.

This thought lifted her spirits somewhat as she came back up the stairs having sorted her mother's tray. By then, John was in bed and had turned on the television. Sara wasn't a fan of having the thing in their bedroom. It was meant to be a place to unwind, not stay up half the night watching films.

Although John rarely came in to see her mother, he knew about her odd habit of repeating syllables. It was cruel of him, but recently he had been laughing about it. 'Pa, pa, pa, pa, pass the remote, will you?' he said to her now. Sara handed it to him, feeling sick. She couldn't even look at him. Michael wouldn't have said such a thing. But then Michael was different. Sara got into bed and turned to face the wall. Michael was different.

7

At work, there was an air of tension, although Sara couldn't put her finger on exactly what it was or why. It was the morning of the meal out and she had gone in early, assuming that, like her, everyone else would be filled with excitement. She planned to get her head down and work through a coffee break if necessary so that she might get away on the dot and enjoy more time getting dressed and straightening her hair. But already, Professor Huxley was in a temper about one of the gastroenterology consultants throwing his weight around over the time they were taking to do some of his samples. Even Dr Bhat, who was usually the picture of serenity, looked hashed. He had a post-mortem booked in and it had been delayed due to some mix-up with the hospital porters.

But it was Michael who was the real shock. Most mornings, he would come into work casually. Often, he turned up quite late. Sara had overheard Dr Bhat mentioning it to the professor once in the corridor. 'Unacceptable' she had heard and 'bad attitude to his work.' Sara's heart rate quickened hearing this. Was Michael really in trouble? She knew that the professor had to sign off his training certificate, but surely the old man wouldn't refuse because of a couple of late starts. She had apologised and squeezed past the two men, unsure why it upset her so much. It was really none of her business at all.

She would often look out for Michael arriving, glancing up from her computer screen if she heard the door at the end of the corridor bang. He would sometimes look into the office and wink, or hold a finger to his lips and pretend to creep past. 'Ridiculous,' Agnes would scold if she saw. 'He's a doctor, for goodness' sake, not some school boy arriving late for class.'

Sara already speculated that Agnes had an axe to grind, although, for what reason, she couldn't say. Jealous, more than likely. She could imagine the old bat having a quiet word with the professor about Michael. Perhaps twisting the knife after he had snubbed her, by saying that he was bad-mannered or tardy in his dictation.

Michael had made it quite clear that the older secretary bored him, completely ignoring her comments over lunch and avoiding any conversation with her if he could help it. Sara had assumed that this was because he preferred to talk to her in the office, but now she wondered if he actively disliked the other woman.

But that morning was different. Instead of his usual panther-like slouch (Sara rather liked this analogy), Michael came right into the office in a bit of a flap. Her smile soon dropped when she saw his bloodshot eyes and lank hair.

'Oh God, Michael, what's happened?'

He glanced across at Agnes who still had her headphones on and refused to look up from her screen. 'Not sure I'll make it tonight. Things have kicked off.'

'Our meal out? But why? What do you mean "kicked off"?'

Michael smiled. 'You're about the only one who would care.'

Sara shook her head in confusion, but also with delight at the compliment. 'You of all people need to have a break,' she said. 'It must be difficult seeing what you see every day. The rest of them are hardened to it.'

Without looking over, Sara knew Agnes would roll her eyes at this, but she didn't care and instead, stayed entirely focused on the young medic who was sighing and rubbing his forehead.

Michael smiled thinly. 'I'm for it.'

'I don't understand... If it's the professor and his research project...'

Michael snorted. 'He can join a long queue of them. God! I don't know why I'm even saying this. I'd better go through and start. You looked up and I couldn't walk past. You always make me feel better.'

Sara shifted in her seat. 'If there's anything I can do? I hope you and Victoria are...'

Michael was moving to the door. He groaned. 'God knows,' he said obscurely. 'God alone knows about Victoria! You're about the only person who looks at me kindly these days. With tenderness. I haven't seen that look in years. Like my own mother.' His hand was on the door. 'It's nice to have one person stick up for me. It's hard enough dealing with them,' he nodded in the lab's direction. 'Day-in, day-out with their petty complaints. Spiteful, most of them and back-stabbing. Don't think I haven't heard,' he said, raising his voice and looking across at Agnes, who still refused to be drawn. 'Stupid bitch,' he hissed.

Sara was horrified, but Michael didn't seem to notice. His eyes wandered around the room as if he was thinking of something else entirely.

'I'll see how the day pans out, and then I'll decide about tonight. Can't see how it can be any fun now though.'

And with that, he left, closing the door with a bang.

Sara's head swam. Of course, it was thrilling that he saw her as a confidante, but what on earth had he meant? Something awful must have happened either at home or in the labs the previous day. She had never seen him look anything other than laid back. She thought of his eyes. They had been so odd, and his demeanour... What was it he had said? He had told her she looked like his mother! That wasn't good. That was appalling. But who had he been talking about when he said they were spiteful and back-stabbing? Sara recalled the odd exchange between him and Hughie only a week before. Was it Hughie who had stirred up trouble for Michael and if so, what had he said? As far as she knew, Michael had only turned up for work late a few times. Other than that, he was an efficient enough doctor. The crumbly old professor and Dr Bhat had no reason to be angry with him.

Sara worried about this a good deal throughout the morning. Agnes announced perhaps it was just as well if Michael didn't come on the work night out anyway, if he was in such ill-humour. Sara had ignored this, and come lunchtime, the department went downstairs together as usual.

'Where's Michael?' she asked Jennifer, looking around as they arrived at the canteen.

'Dr Bhat told him to go home for a bit. Probably be back after lunch, I'd think. They were finishing off the post-mortem together. It was only closing up to do and he must've looked a bit off colour or something. Mind you, his hands were shaking. Wonder if he's run out.'

'Run out? Run out of what?'

Jennifer laughed. 'Are you for real, Sara? You know Michael takes drugs, don't you?'

Sara was speechless.

'Anyway, perhaps he's withdrawing or something. It was very strained this morning.'

'Oh?' Sara asked, now feeling quite sick. What was going on with Michael? How could she not have known?

Jennifer smiled. 'Hullabaloo through the way, there was. Never heard Dr Bhat raise his voice before. Hughie came out, face like thunder too. Have you seen him today, by the way?'

'Hughie? No, why?'

Jennifer grinned. 'You do go around with your head in the clouds, don't you? Black eye.'

'No!'

She nodded.

'What happened?'

'Said he fell over and bumped himself, but he's been jumpy and on edge all morning, so I doubt that. Didn't want to talk to anyone much today.'

'I noticed he was staying behind in the lab instead of joining us for lunch. I assumed it was to sort the samples from the post-mortem.'

Jennifer laughed. 'Sulking, I'd say. He can be a bit like that. Holds a grudge for ages. Both Ettie and I have said it before. If the doctors get annoyed, you take it on the chin. It's part of the job, isn't it? Hughie though, he takes things personally and goodness knows what Dr Bhat made of his appearance when he arrived today. Hardly looks professional does it, turning up with a shiner?'

Sara nodded as they arrived at the canteen.

'Be interesting to see how this evening goes anyway,' Jennifer said, collecting her tray. 'Meant to be a morale booster for the department. Goodness knows how that will work when half of us would rather be anywhere else and the rest are wishing one another dead!'

8

It was with some trepidation that Sara stepped out onto the pavement.

'You don't have to bother. I'll get a taxi home. I don't know what time I'll be,' she said through the open passenger window. John had insisted on driving her despite complaining of an upset stomach.

'Bitter tasting, that penne pasta you gave me,' he had said earlier. 'What was it? A microwave thing?'

'I didn't see the point in cooking up something as it was just you eating. Mum's having scrambled eggs on toast. She only wanted something light.'

This hadn't gone down well. As she did her make-up in the bedroom, she heard him stomping around and the toilet being flushed multiple times. Right enough, when he came in to hurry her along, he did look an awful colour.

'Maybe you should take a tablet to settle you,' she said, nodding to the bedside table.

'Going through my things now, are you?'

She laughed a cold sort of laugh and returned to brushing her hair. Let him have his secrets.

Something had changed that day. She couldn't explain it, but it was to do with Michael. Coming home from work, she had been filled with what could only be described as a sort of new-found feeling of injustice. She had kept silent for too long. Sara had pandered to everyone else's needs, bringing up her family, being the dutiful wife, tending to her ailing mother. But that evening, it was as if she could take it no more. As she went about the house, she felt something deep within her, like the reawakening of what she had once felt when she was young. She laughed aloud as she showered. It was like rediscovering her old self, one who was no longer a downtrodden, fuddy-duddy woman.

Standing naked after the shower, she looked in the mirror. Sara couldn't remember when she had last done that, but she stood there for some time. It was true, her breasts had dropped and her middle had thickened, but her ankles were slight and her upper arms showed none of the awful sag that some poor women of her age seemed to suffer. She stepped closer to the glass to study her face. Her lips weren't as full, and there were more lines around her eyes than when she had last noticed. Sara turned slightly. She still had a nice angle to her jaw and her teeth were even. She could easily give those young lab technicians a run for their money.

Back then, John had thought himself lucky to have her. What made him so cocksure of himself now? She could walk out tomorrow if she wanted to. She wrapped the towel around herself and sighed. That wasn't really true... John had a hold over her that no one else had. Not only was the house in his name, but that, of course, included the granny flat as well. Perhaps she had been naïve allowing him that, but he had built the little annexe himself and as for their home, it had been back in the days when men took responsibility for the house. John had done it as a favour to her, absolving her of accountability. Now, of course, she was utterly trapped.

John must have noticed the new sharpness to her, the edge to her voice. She didn't care. How could he have been married to her for so many years and not have realised?

They were silent in the car. John, because he was sulking, and her, because she was nervous.

Michael had returned to work that afternoon, but she hadn't found a chance to speak to him. In some ways, she was glad. After what he had been like earlier, she wasn't sure she could face him. And now she knew about his addiction, things made more sense – that was if Jennifer's account could be trusted. Sara felt that any solid ground she had once relied on had shifted. Just who could she trust?

It was irrational, but she could pinpoint when the change had happened. It was during her conversation with Michael that morning, something inside her had stirred. People spoke about a curtain lifting when they saw someone in a new light, and she now knew what this meant.

Of course, John was having his issues at work, but that was no excuse. He had essentially abandoned her. Left her to deal with everything alone for what seemed like years.

The more she thought about it, the more convinced she became that her marriage was a sham. She found herself incensed as she thought of how she had allowed herself to become ensnared. How trusting and foolish to end up in a loveless marriage. Was this what it amounted to? She shuddered at the thought. All the while, there was someone who appreciated her. Someone who actually needed her help, but by the laws of convention, she could not offer him the shoulder to cry on that he obviously wanted. No, John had trapped her all right.

Over lunch that day, while the lab technicians chatted to Dr Bhat and the professor, she remained silent. In her mind, she was replaying the conversation with Michael in the office and wishing that she had reached out to him to touch his arm...

John was signalling now, trying to move out into the stream of traffic again as she stood cold on the pavement. He shrugged and looked the other way. 'Whatever, Sara. Do what you want but remember you have to be up for your mother in the morning.'

She turned away. John had driven the fifty yards around the corner so he could pick her up from right outside her mother's front door. She certainly didn't need reminding that she'd have to go over again in the morning. Trapped. Utterly trapped by her marriage and her mother. Why hadn't he helped her? Or even given her a chance to explain how difficult it had become, day-in, day-out. But he hadn't and here she was. It had come to this. If John suggested that she shouldn't drink too much now, he needn't have bothered. Sara knew she needed a clear head.

'I might go out myself for a couple of pints then too,' he shouted after her through the still open window, but she didn't turn and instead marched into the restaurant. In many ways, it felt as if she was setting alight her own funeral pyre and happily stepping into the flames.

Hughie had booked the table, and against Sara's preference, he had gone for Indian. She supposed that the rest of the team had outvoted her. In truth, she didn't much mind, now that it came to it. She doubted she would eat a great deal, anyway.

'Can I take your jacket?' the man at the door asked.

'No, I'd like to keep it.'

She scanned the room, looking for the others. Over the sea of diners busily drinking and eating, she finally saw Dr Bhat's dark head of hair and the professor had spotted her and was raising a hand.

'Over here,' Ettie said, suddenly appearing at her elbow. 'I've just been to the loo. Crowded, isn't it? It's buffet night apparently, so that's why. Are you taking off that big coat?'

'No, I'll hang it on my chair later.'

They zigzagged through the tables to their own.

'Here you are!' Jennifer called, seeing her. 'We were beginning to worry something was up. I know you mentioned your mother, and Agnes was just saying...'

'No, she's fine. I've just come from seeing to her. John drove me here. He's sulking.' She sat down next to Jennifer. 'Hi, Agnes; hi, everyone. You all look very smart. Have you ordered already?' She was being overly cheerful, but it was the only way to cope.

'We were waiting for everyone to come first. Michael's not here and Hughie said he might be a little late too. He had something or other to see to first.'

'What are you drinking, Sara?' Dr Bhat asked, leaning across the table. 'The girls are on white wine, but they're just ordering it by the glass. I could order a bottle if you were...'

'No. No, thank you, not wine.' She looked around the table. Both Dr Bhat and the professor were drinking beer. 'I'll just stick to water just now if that's OK?'

Dr Bhat summoned a waiter, and the glass was beside her within seconds.

'What's everyone eating?' the professor asked, smiling over his spectacles. 'It looks good. I'm wondering about the buffet. What about you, Saj? Are we pushing the boat out and ordering specials or going down the buffet line? You might recommend something. Have you been here before?'

The other doctor grinned and spoke in his soft, affable manner. Sara smiled as he did so. 'No, not before. I'm sure it's all very nice but anglicised to the point of being unrecognisable to anyone of Indian heritage, I'm afraid.'

Jennifer giggled. 'I wasn't that keen either, Dr Bhat. I don't know why Hughie booked it.'

'Who chose then, because I don't like curry?' Sara admitted.

Ettie grimaced. 'Bloody Hughie. He's not even here yet to answer for himself. It would be about right if he bulldozed everyone else's suggestions. I wanted to try that Italian bistro place on the high street. It's been there a while and I've never had the chance to go.'

'Oh well, better not moan too loudly, or they'll blacklist us,' Agnes said.

'I'm thinking buffet,' Ettie said. 'At least you can pick and choose and I've already seen that they have chips.'

Dr Bhat laughed. 'Excellent plan.'

'So, what's the story with John, anyway?' Ettie asked, turning to Sara. 'Why did you say he was sulking?'

Sara grimaced. 'It's not as if I ever really go out, but he's taken umbrage for some reason. Shouted after me that he might be out when I got back, although I can't remember the last time he ever met up with any of his friends.'

'I've got all of this to look forward to then; married bliss.' Ettie sighed. 'That's if it happens at all.'

'How are the wedding plans coming on?'

'Oh, fine, really. I'm doing everything. He's been offshore, and he's taking on extra to pay, he says. I appreciate that, but when he is home, he's never home, if you see what I mean?'

'Who's never home?' Michael asked, grinning down at the table.

Sara looked at Ettie and was puzzled to see she was blushing, but Jennifer was already talking.

'Oh, you made it then, Michael? Come and sit down. What are you drinking? We were waiting for you, and Hughie's still not here. I wonder if he'll explain the black eye after a couple of drinks.'

'Oh, I hope he isn't held up indefinitely.' Michael laughed and winked at Sara.

She looked down at her napkin. Michael was handing one of the waiters his jacket. 'Not ordered a bottle, chaps? God, that's a bit tight. Two of red and two white,' he told the retreating waiter. 'And not the cheap house stuff, either,' he called.

'I don't think anyone else...' began Dr Bhat, but Michael was settling himself and didn't seem to hear.

'How did you end up with an empty seat next to you?' he asked Sara, patting her knee.

She flinched and hoped he hadn't noticed. Across from her, she felt Agnes's eyes on them, and when she looked up, the two lab technicians were staring.

'This keeps happening,' Michael said cheerfully. 'Anyone would think you did it on purpose, Sara. I hoped I'd get beside you for a gossip and not get stuck with some old bore,' he whispered, but the rest of the table must surely have heard. Sara glanced again at Agnes, who had, thus far, said very little as she was being admirably attended to by Dr Bhat. Agnes shook her head. Her mouth was a firm line. Sara looked hurriedly away.

'Really? I wondered if you'd even come tonight, after what you said this morning.'

He looked at her intensely. 'Oh, that?' He laughed. He had already reached the bottom of his glass of red wine and tipped the rest into his throat. 'All forgotten. It's fine and dandy now that we all know where we stand.' He looked around the table challengingly. 'Well, troops, who's up for a deluxe sharing platter to start?'

'I think we're going for the buffet–' began Ettie.

'Nonsense! It's a celebratory meal, a chance for the department to thank their employees, isn't it, Prof?'

The professor looked uncomfortable.

'A platter to begin with, and then individual meals, I say. Is anyone else needing a top-up or am I the only one having?' he asked, holding up the bottle of red.

No one answered.

'Guess it's just me.' He sloshed the burgundy liquid into his glass and raised it. 'Cheers, everyone. To your excellent health, and mine!'

9

Hughie arrived not long after. If things had been strained before, they only became worse when he sat down. Sara thought he looked dreadful. His face was haggard and his hair unkempt. He had changed clothes for the evening, but had a slightly dishevelled appearance, and refused to make eye contact with anyone. No explanation for his lateness was given and when teased about his black eye by Jennifer, he looked furious.

Gradually, the conversation around the table seemed to peter out. Dr Bhat and the professor had tried not to talk shop and had gone through the obvious topics, asking about everyone's partners and what they were planning that summer. Sara felt a pang of guilt for cringing at the old professor and his awkward dialogue.

Beside her, Michael seemed to be only there to get drunk. He had begun the evening by flirting outrageously, but now, had settled into bored silence and between glasses of wine, stared into space across the table. Sara felt sick. She had tried to be quietly attentive, listening to him talking about his old medical school days. She had smiled at the right places, she thought. What had gone wrong? It wasn't like this at work. Then, it was always so easy. All of this felt forced and strange.

Ettie and Jennifer had given up on trying to talk to the rest and were whispering conspiratorially together. Sara couldn't blame them. They were young and shouldn't be here. They should be out dancing or socialising with people of their own age. She wondered if this was what they planned to do following the meal. She had overheard Ettie mentioning a club.

Oddly, the only person who seemed to enjoy themselves was the most reluctant originally to come. Agnes had a slightly spirited appearance about her. When she considered it, Sara knew little about the older woman, other than that she and her husband were keen caravanners and when they both retired, they planned on going on a cruise. Sara had never asked how she had ended up working in the pathology labs. She had been there for some ten years now apparently, but didn't seem fond of the job or the people she worked with. Several times, Sara looked across at her office colleague that evening and saw an odd expression. It was when Agnes was looking at Michael as he downed glass after glass of wine. He was becoming more and more incoherent. *Triumphant*, Sara thought to herself when she looked at Agnes, but why? Had it been her who had stirred up trouble for Michael, and if so, for what reason?

'I need the loo,' Jennifer said after they had finally placed their orders.

'I'll come.' Sara was glad of the excuse to leave the table.

'Bit strained, isn't it?' she asked when both women were standing at the basins, washing their hands.

'I knew it would be like this,' replied Jennifer. 'Work colleagues never end up being friends. Oh, no offence, of course, Sara, but if you look around that table, none of us would choose to spend any more time with one another if we didn't have to.'

'I thought you and Ettie...?'

The younger woman laughed. 'Ettie? No. We get along fine, but we both know where we stand. She's been playing a dangerous game, and she knows I know it. I'm not daft, Sara. If I didn't know a certain something about Ettie, she'd not bother to give me the time of day outside work. Not that I give a hoot one way or another, but it makes things rather interesting, all the same.'

'I don't know what you mean.'

'Probably better that way.' Jennifer glanced sideways at her. 'I've noticed things are a little reserved between you and *him*, by the way.'

'Who?'

'Oh, come on. Don't be silly. Has he fallen out of favour then? I thought tonight would be your big opportunity to get in with him. He's been trying to flirt, but you don't seem so interested. What's up?'

'I think you're drunk.' Sara laughed, but her hands were trembling as she dried them on the paper towels.

'His wife's a bit of a bitch by all accounts, so I'd not be surprised if he tried it on. Fell out this morning, I believe. Not for the first time either. I'm sure there have been plenty of others,' the younger girl said.

Sara was aghast. 'You've got your wires crossed completely. I'm married, and you even suggesting anything of the kind is insulting.'

The younger girl nodded but didn't look convinced. 'Have it your own way.'

They returned to the table. Sara was stony-faced, and her stomach churned. 'Where's my jacket?' she asked.

'Oh, someone knocked it on the floor so I asked the waiter to take it,' said Hughie. 'They hang them all up at the front. You two were an age. Girly gossip, was it?'

Sara swallowed and didn't answer.

'Where's Ettie?' she heard Jennifer ask, but didn't wait to hear the response.

'I'm just going to get something from my coat,' she said to no one in particular and left the table. As she crossed the room, she wondered if she should just go home now. She could easily explain later that she had felt suddenly unwell, or that John had phoned to say that her mother was sick.

She stood by the front door, still undecided. How could she sit at that table knowing that they were all laughing at her? If Jennifer was speaking so openly about her and Michael, then surely the rest were, too. Oh God, how foolish she had been. She had potentially jeopardised her reputation by being silly enough to flirt with a doctor, or not even that, she thought angrily. She had not flirted at all, only allowed herself to be flirted with! It was unfair, so incredibly unfair. Perhaps she should call it a night and go home.

She saw the coat-stand and hunted for her jacket. It had to be there somewhere. She glanced up and through the rain-streaked window, she saw Michael outside on his mobile. He was very drunk now and as he spoke, he staggered up and down on the pavement outside. The door opened, allowing more customers inside. She caught a snatch of what he was saying. 'Where are you? I don't know why you bother. No, no, it's as awful as anticipated.' He laughed. 'I wish I was alone with you, too. Who? Oh yes. Dolled up like nobody's business. God knows why she bothers. I always end up sitting next to her too. Desperate old tart.'

After that, she heard nothing else. She turned from the window, completely numb.

Sara did not leave early that evening, but instead, returned to the table with an icy coolness about her. She sat down and, after taking a moment or two to compose herself, she asked what she had missed. The rest of the group looked at her a little oddly, but she was undeterred and when Michael returned, having finished his telephone conversation, she smiled at him and asked if he'd like some more wine.

10

John looked at her before turning out into the traffic. 'Okay?' he asked.

She had called him from outside the restaurant. The rest had gone on to another pub or club except for Agnes, Dr Bhat, and the professor. Michael could barely walk, and Sara looked at him with both pity and disgust.

'Not joining the youngsters?' Agnes had teased.

Sara shook her head. 'I need to be up early. I don't have the luxury of a long-lie in tomorrow.'

'We can share a taxi?' Agnes offered, but Sara had already called John.

John must have realised that something was wrong. He didn't question her and said that he would be there in five. She knew she didn't deserve it, given how nasty she had been earlier that evening.

He turned up the heater full blast when she got in and said she looked frozen through. It was hard to know what to say. He must surely have expected some explanation, but they sat in silence while he drove, with Sara running over and over the events of that night and what she had just done in her head. It was odd how calculating she had been. A veil of detachment had been draped over her. Funny how seeing John had lifted that. Now, she felt utterly spent. If he was kind to her, she might cry and tell him everything.

'Why are we going this way?' she suddenly asked when she saw he was driving in the wrong direction.

He didn't answer, but she soon realised. She smiled and shook her head, tears pricking her eyes and a lump forming in her throat. 'Idiot.' She laughed. A tear escaped and rolled down her cheek. It was a while since they had laughed and she looked over at his face as he concentrated on the road, his eyes, at times, dazzled by the oncoming headlights of other cars.

'I'm sorry,' she said, and he nodded.

When he stopped the car, now miles from where they lived, they sat together in silence.

'John...' she began.

'Look. They've cut the hedge and put up a bloody big fence,' he said, peering out into the darkness.

'That hedge.' She laughed, glad of the safe ground he had laid for her. 'You should've done the same years ago. The amount of grief it caused you every time cutting the damn thing.'

'I liked it neat,' he replied. 'A fence would have been too easy.'

Sara smiled in the dark. 'Remember the kids in the back garden? It seemed idyllic back then. I wish, sometimes, they hadn't grown up.'

'All things change. Do you regret moving?'

She shook her head. 'It was too big without the girls. No, we did the right thing. Some other family will be enjoying it now.' They sat in silence again until she could bear it no longer. She turned in her seat. 'John, I know I've been a bit...' It was hard to know what she had been. Irritable, selfish, unfaithful? 'Oh, John,' she began again. 'I did something tonight...'

He sighed. 'You don't need to... I don't want to know.'

She tried to gather her thoughts. 'But, John, I think I was mad for a while. It was as if some dreadful cloud came over me.'

'Sara.' He sighed, and she didn't know how to find the words to explain. 'Can we move on? Like we did here.' He gestured to their first house, their family home that still held so many memories of their early marriage and life together. 'I've not changed, you know?' he said, filling the silence. 'I'm the same lad you met all those years ago. I just got bogged down with the building site and, well, I forgot. We both did.'

Sara swallowed. 'John, I need to tell you though...'

'Please don't. If you need to hear it, I forgive you. Please don't say it. It's done. Okay? As long as we agree we are a team now. Is that okay? This is done with now.'

She felt his hand on her arm and in the darkness held on to it tightly.

'I'm sorry,' she mouthed, but he was starting the car.

'A clean sheet.'

She nodded.

He drove them home. She wished she had explained better. But then, what could she have told him, and how would he stay married to her if he knew the extent of it? As they turned the corner onto their street, she was suddenly aware that the haze of burnt-orange street lights had turned to an intermittent blue.

'Shit,' John said, realising perhaps at the same moment that a police car was in their driveway.

He parked half on the kerb and got out.

Sara held on to the car door handle, almost afraid to follow as he marched ahead, up the drive. Oh, God. Her hands shook uncontrollably. It wasn't meant to be like this at all.

When she got out of the car, suddenly afraid of being left

behind, she stumbled, not used to the new high heels. Amid her panic, she had a moment of pure clarity in which she realised John had been her saviour this whole time without her realising it. He would stand by her. John had always been the one.

This only occurred to her for a fleeting second, before the female police officer, having checked Sara's name, told her, with the utmost respect and sensitivity, that her mother was dead.

11

Sara had prepared herself for this moment. It was like she had rehearsed the whole thing. It was strange because she had said goodbye so long ago. None of this should have been a surprise to her. All of those nights she had lain awake imagining how she would react, how she would tell the kids, how they would begin making arrangements. She knew, of course, that John would play an integral role in it. He was good with that sort of thing. If they were in a plane crash, Sara imagined she would perish along with the rest of the poor souls in a screaming panic, but John might stand a chance. He would look for useful options and act with purpose. John would deal with the police now. Why were they there, anyway? None of it was meant to be like this at all.

Sara needed him that night like she never thought she would. Maybe it was the culmination of their marriage. The peak, the pivotal moment. It sounded absurd and horrible to think such a thing. But that evening was when John shone his brightest for her. Their love, in those first dreadful minutes and hours, burned far stronger and more fiercely than the day they married. So good with her, he was. So gentle. He was in the right place, and he said the right things. That night, she needed him, despite not deserving him, and he did not fail her. Thank God he didn't know the truth. Thank God she hadn't told him.

It was difficult to describe, but in those first few minutes, Sara had a strange sensation of watching herself from above. She saw the police officer touching her arm, leading her into the house, followed by John and the other policeman. Her neighbour was there, looking cold and concerned. Sara smiled at her, and the other woman said something, but Sara couldn't quite hear. Her mouth opened and closed like a goldfish, and Sara wanted to laugh. She wondered what her own face was doing. Perhaps she was having a stroke.

Guided by the policewoman, she continued into the house. Her feet were sore, and she thought she kicked off her shoes. She must have done because she was now barefoot. She hadn't painted her toenails in years, but that night she had. She wished she hadn't. A feeling of guilt and shame swept over her. From her position on the ceiling, she saw John talking in the corner of the room with the police. They were saying something about a doctor. Sara couldn't understand what a doctor would do now, but she heard them saying: 'confirm death' and, although she was befuddled, she knew what that meant and nodded. John had one of those air fresheners in his work van. A bulldog that nodded its head when you drove. She thought of it then. Her neck felt floppy. She could nod again and again.

She looked different from above. If helium balloons had eyes, was this what they would see? Bobbing against the ceiling until they ran out of gas. From above, she was prettier than she had realised.

Perfume suddenly filled her nostrils. It seemed to cloud the room. It caught her unaware. Everything was a haze. Perhaps it was the perfume doing it. She knew she could never wear it again, not after that night. Not ever again.

The policewoman brought her a mug of tea. It was in the wrong mug though. One of the posh ones. Sweet, sickly tea. It was the answer to everything, wasn't it? 'I don't know where my jacket is,' she blurted. 'Can you find it? It's important.' The policewoman looked at her with pity, like she had heard or seen this kind of hysteria a thousand times before. Sara couldn't understand why they were being nice to her. 'My jacket,' she kept repeating.

'Take a sip,' the policewoman advised.

As she did so, she plunged back into her body once more. She had to steady herself because of the unexpected jolt. She had preferred it where she had been and felt a little angry. The roof of her mouth was blistered already and she touched the raw ridges with her tongue, feeling the membrane come loose and peel off. The tea made her gag.

She still didn't know what had happened or why the police had been called. For some reason, it didn't even occur to her to ask. Perhaps she was too afraid to hear the answer. It was expected. Phrases like: 'she had a good innings' and 'it was just her time to go,' came into her head. Sara wanted to bat them away like annoying flies. They had no place at a time like that. What was she thinking? She didn't want to accept it as easily as that.

She thought of her father, long since gone, many years ago. Sara almost caught herself looking up, as if searching for him. How stupid. She wondered if there was an afterlife. Would they be meeting up already? She wished she believed in something, but she didn't. Sara felt cheated for not having a faith. She needed one, but she had nothing. Nothing but John. Why wouldn't the rest of them go and leave them be?

Another car was there. She could hear the door slamming. All noises seemed to be fudged together. It was like she was listening through water. But the car door was unmistakable. The girls had had a fish tank once when they lived in the old house on Bridge Street. She had only gone along with it on the agreement that they would clean the thing out. They tired of it pretty quickly and she had allowed the fish to die. She remembered tipping the murky water out. Watching as it slopped against the sink in the kitchen and slugged down the plughole. It left a thick layer of slimy residue on the edge. Sara wondered why she was remembering this. She hadn't thought about the fish in years. She'd need to phone the girls and let them know about their gran.

John had gone outside with one of the police officers. The room was filled with an icy blast of air as they opened the front door. It must be the doctor, someone said. It sounded like something you might hear on a cheap TV comedy, and again she wanted to giggle. 'I'm free!' But no, that was nothing to do with a doctor. That was that department store comedy from God knows how many years back. She was in *EastEnders* years later, the young one. What became of the rest of them? Dead probably. Sara wondered if they were wrong and her mother wasn't dead at all, only unwell. The doctor would know right away. Would she be in trouble? She should never have gone out that night.

She noticed she was rocking back and forward, clutching a cushion. It brought her great comfort, and she felt like she was nursing a small child. Sara missed the closeness, the feeling of being needed. She had had it with her mother for a while before the dementia took hold, and then they were separated by an invisible, rigid curtain. Physical contact was suddenly jarring and awkward.

Did she lie there for long?

Sara thought back to earlier that evening, and when she last spoke with her mother. What had she said to her? What were her last words? Were they the last thing her mother had heard?

Sara didn't even know what she had said. Why hadn't she committed it to memory? It had been such a rush to get out again for her awful meal out. She wished she had never gone.

Did she know she was dying?

Sara tried to visualise her mother's face, but found that she couldn't. She felt annoyed. Cheated. What was wrong with her?

'Did you find my jacket?' she asked again.

Was her mother frightened?

Sara's lips trembled. She was frightened now. She was terribly afraid.

12

'No, I quite understand,' Dr Cathy Moreland said. 'And it was last night? I'll go to speak to the family this morning and discuss the death certificate, that's if you're happy? No reason to think anything untoward had happened? Why was it that you were involved in the first place? Ah, a neighbour. No, that's fine. Yes, it was, perhaps not imminently expected, but certainly not unlikely. We had an anticipatory care plan in place. We've been going in and out. Mainly the district nurses, to be fair.'

She looked out of her window and saw James, her practice partner, crossing the car park to the back door, having just been out to an early visit. He spotted her by the window and raised a hand. Cathy grinned and rolled her eyes, pointing to the telephone. He nodded and disappeared, his suit jacket flapping in the wind. The back door banged.

'Was it one of the out-of-hours doctors who attended?' she asked. 'Of course. And the son-in-law identified her? I can speak to the procurator fiscal if you'd like too but it seems straightforward enough.'

Cathy moved the receiver to hear better and James appeared

at her door, looking windswept but cheerful. He mouthed 'Okay?' and she nodded.

'I'll be putting Alzheimer's on the death certificate, yes. If she was found on the floor, possible stroke as the primary cause.'

James, who had continued to hover in the doorway, grimaced and then quietly closed the door as he left. She'd catch up with him later. Sometimes, it could be like that. They could go for a full day without speaking. She returned to her call.

'I assume that the daughter– Yes, I can imagine. I know her reasonably well and she does seem that way. I think she has family around her– Oh, that's fine, and he's with her, is he? Good. No, that's no bother at all. Another job to add to my list, but I'll happily see to it later today. No, thank you for letting me know. I'm sorry that you were involved at all. Goodbye.'

She replaced the receiver and sighed. Next door, she could hear James switching on lights, his computer, and then running a tap. They were both stretched. There seemed to be an ever-increasing list of jobs to do that day. Coffee was now out of the question.

So Mrs Golding had died. Not a bad thing in some ways, Cathy reflected as she typed up her previous patient's notes. With the interruption of the phone call from the police, she had forgotten some of her examination findings, and she had to sit for a moment or two to think. Oh yes, she remembered now. She quickly completed the consultation on the computer and lapsed back into her chair. She'd not been out to see poor Mrs Golding for some time, but Iris, their district nurse, had spoken about her only the other day at their multidisciplinary team meeting.

Cathy added the family to her list of house visits and got up. Her back ached, and she stretched her hands high above her head. She'd been sitting hunched at the computer for too long. It was a relief to leave her room and, with a legitimate excuse to do so, she jogged along the corridor, enjoying the cool air from

the back door as it hit her. At the top of the stairs, she tapped on
the door. Already, she had the end of her surgery to see to and
then four visits booked in so she'd have to be quick.

'Come in,' called a voice.

Iris was sitting at a desk with her hand clasped over the
receiver of her phone. 'One minute,' she mouthed, and Cathy
nodded and smiled. She listened to Iris ably managing what
sounded like an irate caller.

'One of us will be in by the end of the week,' the other
woman promised. 'No, maybe not myself, but...' Iris grinned at
Cathy. 'Yes, I understand that, but I can't promise to always be
the one out every time. Tell her I'll try my best, is that all right?
Okay, take care then.' She replaced the phone and sighed.

'One of those days?' Cathy asked, and came into the room.

'Honestly, it's not stopped all morning. I suppose you've
heard about Mrs Golding?'

Cathy smiled. 'That's why I came up. I just had the police on
the phone.'

'Police? But there wasn't anything suspicious, was there? Had
she fallen? I'd only heard that she died in the night.'

'No, nothing like that. I think a concerned neighbour heard
noise from inside the house. Mrs Golding would usually be in
bed early and presumably, they heard something. Perhaps it was
her falling over. Apparently, the neighbour tried knocking on
the daughter and son-in-law's door to check, but they weren't in,
so they went around the house and saw Mrs Golding lying on
the living room floor, poor thing.'

'Oh, God. What a shame. Had she passed away then?'

'I think so. The police broke in and not knowing the
situation, I think one of them had started CPR.' Cathy grimaced.

'Oh no.' Iris covered her face with her hands. 'But our
anticipatory care plan. All that work.'

'Quite. Especially upsetting after the conversation I'd had

with the daughter only recently about signing the DNR. That was bad enough and to have the police performing heroics, too.'

'Did they call the ambulance too, then?'

'Yes, but thank God someone saw sense and stopped.'

Iris sighed. 'All that work we put in preparing for the end of her life, and then that happens. No dignity to it. I hope the daughter isn't annoyed. I remember she was a bit odd with you when you spoke to her about it all.'

Cathy perched on the edge of Iris's desk, dislodging a couple of folders that fell to the floor. She stooped to retrieve them. 'Yes, she was a little strange. She needed little persuasion about the Do Not Resuscitate form. Maybe I caught her on a bad day. Who can blame her, though? It must have been difficult watching her mother deteriorate. In some ways, this will come as a great relief to her.'

'I spoke with her last week and she seemed to be coping, although the incontinence was becoming more frequent. She'd never been keen on the nursing home suggestion though, but I said to her it was becoming a concern for us going in.'

'What did you think about the daughter?' Cathy asked. 'I'll have to go out later and see her. She's a medical secretary up at the hospital, I believe?'

'Yes. Seems professional and all that. Bit intense and liked to read about things. She's asked me a lot of tough questions over the months. I had a rather uncomfortable conversation with her once, right back at the beginning, about euthanasia. It was a while back, but it's always hard when people mention things like that, even just in passing...'

'Yes, she said something ambiguous about it to me as well. Oh, dear.' Cathy shifted from her position on the desk and stood once more.

'Well, exactly.' Iris nodded, looking up at her. 'But as you say, it must have been hard to watch her mother decline so rapidly...'

'Okay, well, I'll go out later today and see them. Thanks.' Cathy descended the stairs once more and reluctantly returned to her room to continue consulting. Several times, she heard James talking in the room next door. She was just seeing her final patient out when her phone rang.

'Michelle?' she asked, seeing that the call had come from reception.

'Sorry. I just saw you'd finished your last one and wanted to catch you before you headed out. Visits are stacking up, aren't they?'

'Nightmare,' Cathy agreed.

The lead receptionist cleared her throat. 'I saw you'd put Mrs Golding's daughter in for a visit. A Mrs Sara Wiseman?'

'Yes. I'm heading over there, after the two on the other side of town and then Mr Stoneleigh. It's in that direction, anyway.'

'I've had the husband on the phone just now. He wanted to speak to one of the doctors urgently. I told him they were down for a visit already and that seemed to pacify him, but he sounded in a bit of a state. I thought I should warn you at least. Might be a tricky one.'

'Did he say anything else? I wasn't racing to them first because it's a bereavement visit and I didn't want to be looking at the clock thinking I had another three to do afterwards.'

Michelle sounded uncertain. 'Obviously, I couldn't ask what it was all about. It sounded a bit more than just the wife being upset. Maybe you should ring him before going? I took his mobile number just in case.'

Cathy sighed. 'Go on,' she said and Michelle read it out.

There was no answer when she rang. Cathy tutted. What could be so urgent, anyway? She was going out later. To rearrange her visits was completely unnecessary, and whatever the son-in-law of Mrs Golding had to say to her, would have to wait. Nothing could be that pressing.

As Cathy turned her car out onto Ancrum Road, her phone buzzed. She glanced down, but the caller had withheld their number. She'd already wasted enough time that morning, so as long as it wasn't the practice trying to get hold of her, she'd leave it.

Her first three visits took longer than she had expected. By the time she turned into the cul-de-sac to perform her final visit of the day, she was feeling frazzled. She took a moment to compose herself, knowing that Mrs Golding's daughter might well be distressed by what had happened the night before.

Getting out of the car, she looked up and saw a tall man in jeans and T-shirt hovering by the front door. The husband, she assumed. She didn't even know his name. That wasn't a brilliant start.

Cathy smiled at him as she walked up the drive with her doctors' bag in hand. 'I'm so sorry,' she said.

He seemed agitated, and beckoned for her to come to the side of the drive.

'I wanted a word before you went in. I tried to call but couldn't get you. Something's wrong. Very wrong. I think...' the man glanced over towards the open door. 'I think the way she's been talking this morning; she might need a sedative.'

'Oh?'

'I think she's having a breakdown.'

Cathy didn't understand. 'But, Mr Wiseman...'

'John,' he told her.

'John, grief can affect people in different ways. Her mother had been failing for some time, but to die unexpectedly...'

He shook his head. 'It's nothing to do with her mother. It's not that at all. She was in shock last night, of course. We had a long chat, and she agreed it was a blessing. After the police left, she slept better than she's done in weeks. No, it was this morning when she heard the other news...'

Cathy shook her head. 'I don't understand.'

'The phone rang first thing. She'd been on a work night out last night. That's why we weren't at home when her mother was found. I went to pick her up. We needed to talk.'

Cathy waited.

'Anyway, she had a call this morning. One of her colleagues... Seemingly, one of the people who had been with her yesterday evening... Apparently, he's been found dead.' Mr Wiseman leaned in towards her. 'I feel terrible saying it, and believe me, I wouldn't if I wasn't so concerned. Yesterday evening, before all of this kicked off with her mother, she was cut up about something. She phoned from the restaurant, wanting me to collect her. I knew something was wrong then. But now, the way she's carrying on blaming herself, you'd think she'd had a hand in this man's death.'

13

Sara Wiseman was on the sofa. She didn't look up when Cathy came into the room, but clung onto a cushion, holding it close to her chest. Cathy saw her knuckles were as pale as her face. She looked utterly worn.

'Mrs Wiseman? May I sit down?'

Her husband came into the room also and answered for his wife, sounding overly cheerful. 'Of course, you can, doctor. Over there.' He indicated a large comfortable-looking armchair.

'Sara, I'm sorry to hear about your mother. Last night sounds like it was a dreadful shock for you. I hear you and...' She turned and looked at Mr Wiseman. 'You and John were out that evening? It must have been a frightful thing to return to.'

The woman cleared her throat, but when her words came, they were still rasping, as if she'd not spoken aloud for some time. 'I was out. John came to pick me up. Yes, a shock.'

Cathy glanced at Mr Wiseman.

'I've told the doctor about your work colleague also, Sara. It's been a bit of a double-whammy for you today.'

The woman smiled slightly, and her face then fell back to gaunt fatigue. Cathy had met her a couple of times before, but she seemed to have aged since then. Perhaps it had happened overnight. Grief could do strange things and its impact could be quite physical.

She shifted in her seat. 'I'm so sorry,' she repeated. 'Two bereavements in such a short space of time is very difficult.' She paused, but Mrs Wiseman didn't speak. 'The reason I came today was to see how you were, of course, but also, I wanted to talk to you about your mother's death certificate.'

'The police said that you would.' Mr Wiseman nodded.

Cathy turned. 'I wanted to discuss her cause of death...'

'Alzheimer's,' Mrs Wiseman said. 'That bloody disease took everything.'

'I will put it on the form, of course, but they found her lying on the floor, I believe?'

Mrs Wiseman looked up sharply. 'Yes? And what of it?'

'Well, I could put general frailty as the cause of death, but it's not quite right. Although we had discussed her care provisions a good deal as she was declining, I didn't expect her to pass away so rapidly.'

'Are you accusing me of killing her?' Mrs Wiseman snapped.

'Oh, my goodness, no!' Cathy was aghast.

'Well, what is it you're saying? She had to die somewhere, and it happened to be on the floor. I was out. John was out. Not that he matters in all of this.'

Cathy looked desperately across at Mr Wiseman, horrified by this sudden change in manner.

'Sara, the doctor isn't accusing you of anything. She's trying to help. Isn't that right?'

'Yes, that's right. This may seem odd, I appreciate that, but I often discuss this with families. Frequently, in cases such as this, I'll put stroke as the first cause of death, with Alzheimer's and frailty as secondary causes. That was what I wanted to discuss with you today. Not to accuse you of anything. Surely the police clarified they were in no doubt that your mother had died of natural causes?'

Mrs Wiseman's face, although still wan, showed two patches of red, high on her cheeks. 'Of course,' she said.

Cathy wasn't convinced they were on the same page and turned to Mr Wiseman.

'You must forgive us, doctor. It's been a terrible night,' he said and looked hard at her as if trying to subliminally communicate something of great importance.

Cathy nodded, still unsure, but turned back to his wife. 'You've been under a good deal of strain caring for your mother these past few months. I spoke with Iris, our district nurse before I came out to see you. She said that it had been hard more recently. The incontinence had been worse? I hope we supported you enough?'

'It's a relief,' the other woman said savagely. 'I sound callous saying it, but it's true all the same. No one should have to watch someone they love go through that. She had no idea who I was at the end. No idea who she was even.'

'I am sorry. You're right. It's a horrible disease. I wish I could have made it easier.'

Mrs Wiseman shook her head. 'I don't care what you put on the damn certificate. None of it matters. Put stroke, myocardial infarction, pulmonary embolus...'

'Of course, you are a medical secretary.' Cathy was glad of the opportunity to change the subject. 'Where is it you work, remind me?'

'Pathology,' she answered, and then let out a shuddering gasp.

Her husband went to her. Sara's face had crumpled, and she pummelled the cushion she was holding. 'Oh, God! Michael, why?' she moaned. Her husband reached out to comfort her and she turned on him like a wild animal. 'Don't touch me, John! No one touch me. You don't understand. None of you understands.' She turned to Cathy, her eyes narrowed and full of pain. 'I'm glad my mother's dead! There, I said it. Glad. It's a relief to have it over. But not him. It shouldn't have happened to him. Not Michael. It was a mistake. I wish it had been me instead. I wish I was dead.'

And then she collapsed against her husband and sobbed inconsolably.

14

'Cath? What's up? You sound funny.'

Cathy sighed. She had returned to the practice, having finally left Mr and Mrs Wiseman in what she thought was a worse state than when she had first gone in. Strange for Mrs Wiseman to be so defensive, firstly, about her mother's cause of death, and then to act so hysterically about her colleague. It did all seem rather odd.

'I'm sorry to phone out of the blue,' Cathy told her friend. The first thing she had wanted to do, though, was check. 'Suz, tell me to mind my business, but I just wanted to see if Saj was okay? He didn't happen to be on a work night out last night, did he?'

'I don't know how you do it! So, you've heard about it already, but how?'

Cathy sighed. 'I had a horrible feeling when she said it was a pathology department meal out. So, Saj was there, was he? I assume he knew the man who died? I believe it was someone called Michael, but I don't know any more than that?'

'Yes. Michael was one of the medical registrars. He's been attached to the department these past three months or so. Saj wasn't especially close to him. Shocking all the same. A young doctor. Funny, intelligent. Promising career ahead of him too. But how have you heard about it?'

'A patient. I've just done a bereavement visit.'

'Oh, God. Not one of Michael's family? I didn't realise he was from the area.'

'No. That's the odd thing. The woman I was seeing was down for a bereavement visit this morning because her mother died last night. She had Alzheimer's, so it wasn't wholly unexpected.'

'What's she got to do with Michael, then?'

'Well, she was upset about her mother, of course, but she was far more saddened to hear of the death of her colleague, Michael. She's one of the pathology secretaries. Presumably Saj will know her quite well. She was at the meal last night too.'

Suzalinna exhaled. 'Small world. I don't suppose you think there was something iffy about the whole thing, do you?'

'Why do you say that?'

Her friend laughed. 'There always is when you're involved! Another little mystery for Dr Cathy Moreland to solve? Darling, if there is, can I be part of it this time? I know you like to keep these things to yourself, but I've been dying for a bit of intrigue. As it happens, work's been an absolute bore. We've taken on a couple of new registrars who are incredibly efficient for a change, but it does mean that I rarely get a look-in. I'm glad they are so competent, of course. They will make excellent accident and emergency consultants. But it is a bit dull. I've been stuck in my office these past few shifts doing bloody paperwork, willing my bleep to go off, but it never does. No one needs me. Last week, we got called out in the helicopter but they were all over that too.'

Cathy laughed. 'I assume this Michael chap didn't go through your department last night, then? Do you know anything about how he died? I've got no details at all.'

'I'm waiting for Saj to come back. He's been away for hours. Police station. I suppose they're interviewing all the folk who were at the dinner. All I know is that a neighbour called an ambulance when Michael arrived home, but they didn't even take him. He was obviously past the point for any heroics, and it looked odd. I guess they called the police right away.'

'Where did they go last night, anyway?'

'What, for the meal? Rishis in town. Not somewhere we've ever been before, but all the same, you'd hardly expect to collapse and die after eating there. Maybe they'll shut the place. Right enough, Saj had an upset stomach this morning. I wonder about the rest of the department. This woman you just saw, did she have any symptoms of food poisoning?'

'Well, no, but then, I wasn't asking about her bowel habit. It was all rather uncomfortable as it was.'

'I bet we'll be disappointed and the police surgeons will find an undiagnosed aneurysm on post-mortem. When Saj gets back, I'll get him to call you, will I?'

'Thanks, please do. I'd be interested to hear. If I don't pick up, it's because I'm consulting and I'll get back to him later. Listen, I'd better get on,' Cathy said, glancing at the clock and seeing that her next patient would be due soon.

'Hang on, you've not promised yet.'

'Promised what?'

'That I'm in on it too, if it turns out to be one of your mysteries. Say it, darling. I need some excitement. Say it please.'

Cathy laughed and hung up.

She didn't hear from Saj until that evening. Cathy wondered if he might not call at all, but when her mobile lit up, she snatched at it, keen to hear what he had to say. Mrs Wiseman had been on her mind for most of that day and Cathy couldn't shake from her memory those words: *It shouldn't have happened to him. Not Michael. It was a mistake.* Just what had Mrs Wiseman meant? Was it shock, or had it been more?

'Sorry,' he said. 'It's been a bit of a day. Are you all right to talk just now? Suz said you'd called earlier.'

'Oh, you sound exhausted. Yes, I'm fine to talk. Did Suzalinna explain my interest? One of my patients from this morning is a member of your team. A Sara Wiseman? I did a house call to her. Bereavement visit.'

'Yes. She's one of the secretaries. Suz said that her mother died last night as well. What a dreadful evening. She must be in a terrible state.'

'She is. But did Suzalinna also tell you that Sara seems far less upset about her mother than she is about Michael?'

Saj sighed.

Cathy had known him and Suzalinna for years. They had been so supportive to her throughout her own troubled times. Both friends had accompanied her to hospital appointments. Suzalinna supplied the positive chatter, and Saj the gentle reassurance. Cathy had needed both when she was diagnosed with bipolar disorder. They had stood by her when many others had not.

Cathy grimaced, recalling the variety of responses she had received when she told people she was taking time off work for both her own and her patients' safety.

One friend had laughed. 'I wondered, you know, when you suggested going out for a meal and staying in a hotel in town? I thought it was extravagant and now we know why! God! What a state you were in. You probably can't remember?' Cathy hadn't bothered to explain that no, she had been quite 'normal' when she had suggested it. It wasn't the bipolar talking at all. She would be unlikely to ask again, though.

At the other end of the scale, her parents had been more nonchalant. 'Everyone has it these days,' her father had said. 'It's the hip new thing. Just about every arty-farty sort has some mood disorder or mania.' Her mother had been in denial. 'We all have our ups and downs, darling,' she had said. Only when Cathy was admitted to the psychiatric ward, did they finally realise the seriousness of the situation.

But Suzalinna and Saj had been there for her, expecting nothing in return and offering no more than she wanted or needed. They were on her side, and she'd be forever grateful for that.

Saj sighed again. The strain of the last day must have taken its toll.

'This thing with Michael and Sara,' he began. 'There's been a bit of a rumour about the two of them. I didn't know anything about it until last night at the meal. You know fine well that people don't come to me with gossip and I'm too busy at work to notice these things, but a few remarks over the dinner did make me think.'

'An affair? Gosh, I'm surprised. I'd have thought Sara was too caught up caring for her dementing mother to have time for that. And with a doctor too?'

'I don't know if it's true. Michael was like that anyway. Very flirtatious with every woman he spoke to. He probably thought that it was quite normal to talk to people like that. Maybe Sara read something more into it. I don't know. This is all conjecture.'

'So, what are the police saying? I assume they're waiting on a PM?'

'Yes. It sounds odd. When I heard the news, I thought it must have been a sudden MI. He was drinking heavily last night so I wondered too if he'd fallen on the way home and given himself a subdural. They went to a club afterwards, a couple of the lab technicians and him. I headed home, along with the rest of the old fogies. I'm past all that nonsense now and Suz was waiting up.'

'So, what happened, then?'

'It seems that he arrived home on his doorstep in a bit of a mess. His wife, Victoria, who's actually an ENT nurse, panicked a bit. I think he vomited a couple of times and she saw traces of blood. Apparently, it was a neighbour who heard the commotion and phoned the ambulance, but by the time they got to him, he was dead.'

'Strange,' Cathy said. 'But I still think it sounds like natural causes, don't you?'

'Well, yes and no. It doesn't really fit with sudden death syndrome, an arrhythmia or anything that you'd expect in someone so young. As it happens, I spoke to the doctor on call for the police. He wasn't thrilled with the whole thing. He said he didn't like the look of it. You know what it's like? You get a bit of a hunch about things. He said he'd do the post-mortem and then know, but he felt it wasn't adding up.'

'I guess we just wait to hear then.'

Saj sighed. 'Indeed. An awful end to what had been a difficult week already.'

'Have things been bad at work generally?'

'Yes. That was what this silly meal out was for, to boost staff morale. Now, one of our team is dead.'

'Oh, Saj, I'm sorry.'

'It is what it is. The labs are busy. Everyone is narky. Michael, although I hate to say it now that he's dead, but he was a challenge.'

'How so?'

'Both the professor and I had some concerns about his work ethic from the start, and then, someone made a complaint. I'll not bore you with the details, but it was all a bit frosty between us this past week or so. I'm horrified to hear that he's died, but I must say, the department will be a lot more settled without him there.'

'Are you worried about it being suicide?'

'If I'm honest, I wasn't before I spoke with the police surgeon, but now, perhaps...'

'Listen, Saj, I'll let you go. You sound like you need a stiff drink and off to bed. If you do hear anything...'

'You'll be the first to know, of course. Well, after Suz, obviously. She tells me she's helping you out on this one if it turns out to be foul play?'

Cathy laughed. 'I hope it doesn't come to that.'

'You and me both, Cathy. You and me both.'

15

Cathy stood at the kitchen window and looked out at the blue-black of the night sky. She knew what Saj meant. Without question, if it did turn out that Michael had died of anything other than natural causes, it would be an ordeal.

She crossed the kitchen. Absent-mindedly, she turned on the tap and held the kettle to it. What Saj had said was concerning. She knew that he, along with the rest of the pathology team, might take the burden of Michael's death on their shoulders if it turned out that he had committed suicide. And that now seemed a possibility.

What had Saj said about Michael being a challenge? Had the young registrar realised that he was in trouble with his supervisors? Had this threat pushed an already concerned man over the edge? Cathy shook her head. Not from what she had heard of Michael. He sounded like he had been a bit of a player. Saj had told her that there had been rumours about him and Sara Wiseman, his medical secretary. Someone like that who, despite being married and settled, was hardly the sort to become upset about their seniors bad-mouthing them. Certainly not to the extent that they would take their own life.

'He'd have left a note,' Cathy said to herself. 'Medics like things to be tidy,' and then, realising that the kettle was now full almost to the brim, she tipped out most of the water and blotted the side with a tea towel, resting it back on its cradle and flicking the switch.

Admittedly, with access to a multitude of hazardous chemicals in a laboratory setting, Michael had the means to do it, but it didn't add up. Why do it on a night out with the rest of the team? The unhappy stories that she had heard of medics deciding to kill themselves mostly ended in a locked office with an injection of diamorphine, or in deserted woodland with a meticulously tied noose.

Of course, he might have taken something deliberately, not meaning to kill himself. More and more junior doctors were taking pep-pills to keep themselves awake during long shifts. Only recently, she had read an article in the medical journal about the increasing trend. Drug misuse amongst doctors had been a long-standing issue. With access to drugs and the knowledge of how they might affect them, medics sometimes walked a dangerous line.

But then, it might be none of those things. Michael might have died of an arrhythmia or aneurysm. He might have had some pre-existing illness that none of the pathology team was aware of. The police surgeon that Saj had chatted to might well have been bragging. After all, you couldn't have a hunch about someone's cause of death, could you?

'You're as bored as Suzalinna,' Cathy said to herself, pouring the now-boiled water into her mug of powdery chocolate. 'Bored and looking for trouble and that's the last thing poor Saj needs.' She stirred the dark liquid around and around, smelling the sickly aroma.

Why did Sara Wiseman blame herself then? And what was the complaint made about Michael that Saj had mentioned?

'Stop it,' she told herself. 'It's none of your business. A tragic death of a fellow doctor, but none of your business at all.' It was just circumstances that had put her into the story. Had Sara not been her patient, she'd have heard on the grapevine about it no doubt, but not been involved in the slightest.

But you are involved, a voice in her head said. *And you will await the post-mortem results with more eagerness than you should.*

Cathy stirred the hot chocolate vigorously. It slopped up the edge of the mug and splashed on the kitchen worktop.

She had to wait the whole of the next two days and then half of the following until she heard any more about Michael Croft's death. She'd not known his surname before, but that was what he was called. Dr Croft. 'A promising young doctor,' the email said. It wasn't unusual for notices such as these to go into the trust's general mail. Usually, the obituaries were for doctors who had reached what might be deemed a reasonable age. Poor Michael Croft was only twenty-eight. It seemed all the more appalling that such a thing had happened. Of course, the email said nothing about the cause of death. As far as Cathy was aware, at that point anyway, none had been established. These things took some time if it wasn't a clear-cut case. She was sure that if any news had emerged, Saj would have told her straight away.

One thing she did learn from the email, though, was that Michael was childless but left behind a widow, Victoria. Cathy recalled what Saj had said. She was an ENT nurse apparently and had panicked somewhat when her husband returned home.

Little wonder, Cathy thought. She'd sent her husband out for an evening of drinks and fun, only to have him return, dying on her doorstep.

Cathy had stopped snatching up her mobile every time it buzzed, and when Saj did eventually try to call her, she ignored the phone, leaving it vibrating in her pocket until she had finished in a meeting with the multidisciplinary team.

'Sorry I missed you, Saj, I was in a meeting. Any news?' she asked, back downstairs in her consulting room with the door firmly closed.

'Yes,' he said. 'I'm afraid there is, and it's not what I, or anyone, wanted to hear. Listen, I'm at work, Cathy. I can't talk much. Maybe it's better if you come over this evening for dinner, anyway. Then I'll tell you the full story.'

'Saj!' she said. 'You can't leave me waiting all day.'

He laughed, but she could hear how strained he was. 'Non-accidental,' he said shortly. 'But now a note has been found. Really, Cathy, I can't say any more just now. Come over to ours this evening. I'll cook something. Suz will be delighted. Come at seven and we'll talk.'

'Okay,' she said. 'I'll come. You're all right, are you?'

'I need to go,' he told her, and the phone went dead.

Cathy had a full surgery of patients booked in that afternoon, but it was more than a little difficult to concentrate, knowing how upset her friend was. It now seemed clear from what he had said that Michael had taken his own life, though. How utterly dreadful. And he had left a note. Had he explained in it why he had chosen that way out? Cathy hoped that his work hadn't been mentioned. She knew how this might impact the pathology lab and how that, in turn, would concern Saj. An enquiry would be unavoidable, of course, and rightly so. But if anyone in the lab was implicated in encouraging or contributing to Michael's desperate final act, they would not go unpunished.

She recalled Sara Wiseman's words: 'I wish it had been me.' Cathy thought of Saj and hoped that his name wasn't in the note. Anything but that, she prayed. He's too kind a person to be involved at all. She looked up at the clock. Four and a half hours and she'd hear the full story. Until then, she'd have to forget about Michael Croft and concentrate on her patients. But, of course, it wasn't so simple.

'You never even met the man,' she told herself. 'And yet, he's got under your skin.'

16

She arrived at seven. Saj came to the door.

'Sorry about earlier,' he said, and kissed her cheek. His lips felt cool. 'Bad time. Come in. She's through there. She's already started on the wine.' He nodded over his shoulder and Cathy saw her friend in the kitchen, grinning. She wore a beautiful sequin top, which caught the light and made Cathy squint.

Cathy removed her jacket and hung it on the end of the stairs.

'I can't join her on the booze, I'm afraid. I brought the car. How are you, Saj? You sounded dreadful on the phone.'

They walked through to the kitchen, and before he could answer, Suzalinna had enveloped her in a hug. 'Darling! What a treat, and on a school night too. So glad you came. I'm off tomorrow so I've started a bottle. You'll have one to keep me company, won't you?'

'Driving,' Cathy said again, and grimaced. 'I'm in first thing. I'll have water if that's okay?'

Saj had already got it for her and was handing her the glass. She smiled her thanks.

'You look gorgeous by the way, Suz, you always do in your sparkly things. So, a bit of a horrible start to the week?'

'Well, it's been all weekend really for us,' Suzalinna said. 'Poor old Saj didn't know what to do with himself, did you? You'd have thought he'd be better adjusted to death, what with his line of work, but you're not, are you, Saj darling?'

Her husband had returned to stirring something on the stove. He frowned. 'Not when it's someone I actually know.'

'Nightmare,' Suzalinna mouthed and took a swig of her wine. 'We'll go through to the front room, will we? You can tell Cathy the details over dinner, Saj. Come on, darling. He's in a grump with me at the moment. Says I'm enjoying it all too much. But like I said to you before, life is very dull for me. I need a bit of intrigue, and it's not as if Saj liked this chap. Sure, they worked together, but they weren't exactly close.'

Suzalinna led her through to the living room. It was a beautiful house and her friend had furnished it immaculately. Small touches reflecting her Indian upbringing were everywhere. The silk cushions of deep jewel colours casually scattered on the rattan chairs at the far end of the room, the ornately carved wooden elephants lined up in order of size on the mantelpiece. Cathy flopped down in the chair that she had so often sat in.

'So?' she began.

'Well,' Suzalinna said, rather too gleefully. 'He's been like a bear with a sore head all weekend. Honestly, I'm glad you've come. You'll get him out of his mood and he'll have to be polite. I know he's upset but he'll tell you himself that this registrar was a dreadful worry. Both he and the professor had raised concerns.'

'Professor...?'

'Huxley. Old boy. You've heard Saj mention him before, no doubt. Saj's mentor, I suppose you'd call him, although they are as qualified as one another now. The professor's done a bit of research too, of course. He took Saj under his wing when he first came over from India to start work. Remember Saj had done his house jobs back home? He was all set to specialise and for God knows what reason, set his heart on pathology. Boring as hell, if you ask me. I always hated histology at medical school. Pink and purple blobs under microscopes. Not my idea of fun!'

Cathy laughed.

'Anyway, Huxley mentored Saj through his college exams. Saw great potential in him, obviously, and rightly so. As you know, Saj aced all the assessments and got the highest grades. Even so, he was lucky to get the consultant position here. They essentially invented the post for him. Now, he's the prof's right-hand man.'

'But this Michael chap...'

'Michael Croft. Yes, he came to the department as part of one of these silly new rotation things that the deanery has set up. Some of the medics who have expressed a specific interest in pathology and research, get to work in the lab for part of the year. Like bloody work experience, and a bit of a skive by all accounts. Some of them see it that way and hang around like silly school kids, doing next-to-nothing. The department only has one registrar at a time. It's a busy lab and Saj and the professor don't have time to supervise more when they're doing their own work as well.'

'And Michael? Was he the type to get stuck in, or did he act like a school leaver?'

Suzalinna scrunched up her nose. 'You'll have to pump Saj for the low-down I suppose on that, but I know for a fact that it wasn't just the one night that Saj came home ill-tempered because of him.'

'Oh?'

'To be fair to Saj, he's a very serious, dedicated sort. You know how much he loves his job? It's his vocation, really. God knows how bad this young fellow actually was at his work, but Saj used to be upset some nights. Not turning up on time, screwing up some of the samples, ordering the wrong chemicals. That sort of thing.'

'Had they spoken to him about it? I assume if a registrar attached to the department isn't pulling their weight, or is causing them difficulty, the deanery would have to be informed and some kind of warning given?'

'I don't think the prof had gone that far yet. Things got worse though last week. Something to do with a research project that the professor's been working on for some time. The registrars usually help out with that side of things. If they're any good, they get their name on a paper and the professor often gets published in quite well-thought-of medical journals. I think things went wrong there though. They might have allowed Michael to cruise through the last few months of his rotation without making a complaint, but he was horribly arrogant and argumentative. Made trouble amongst the technicians. I don't know the ins and outs, of course. Saj'll explain though, won't you, Saj?'

Saj had come into the room. He held a tea towel and a glass of red wine and already the tension was gone from his face.

'Food's nearly ready if you want to come through,' he said. 'Then, I'll give you the real facts, instead of Suzalinna's exaggerated version.' He grinned at his wife, for the first time showing the playfulness that Cathy knew so well.

'Beast,' Suzalinna said and held out a hand to him. He crossed the room and hauled her up out of her chair.

'You embellish horribly,' he scolded. 'I've told you off about it before.'

Suzalinna giggled. 'Come on, Cath. Are you ready to hear the truth, as Saj sees it, then?'

The meal was just a family staple, as Saj called it, but the curry was incredibly fragrant and good.

'Mum used to make this when we had exams,' he laughed. 'She said it was brain food. Have you got enough rice, Cathy?'

She told him she had. 'So, Saj...'

'Yes, I realise you're keen to know about it. I got a call from my pathology friend.'

Cathy looked confused.

'The police surgeon. He shouldn't really have spoken to me, but we know of one another and he was really doing it out of courtesy. Giving me a heads-up so I could prepare myself for the police interrogations, perhaps.' He laughed, but his face quickly returned to seriousness. 'He was right about Michael when he said he had a hunch something was wrong. The police already told him to look for anything untoward. They found a note explaining that he was ending it. I don't know the details of that, of course. Michael didn't go into the whys and wherefores, as far as I'm aware, but my friend said he wasn't surprised by his preliminary findings. He had already sent away stomach contents samples assuming poisoning whether it be accidental or non.'

'What had he taken?'

'This is the worst bit. It would almost be easier if it was something well-known. It seems that he'd taken a preservative compound. Sodium Azide. Highly toxic stuff. Something that joe-public wouldn't readily have access to. Horrible way to do it, as it happens. Horrible.'

'Was it from the lab, Saj? Was that where he'd found this chemical?'

Saj laid down his fork and sighed. 'There was a mix-up with

an order the previous week. One of our suppliers sent the wrong strength of chemical and it was meant to be returned. Sodium Azide is a bacteriostatic compound. It inhibits cytochrome oxidase in gram-negative bacteria. I've been into the lab over the weekend. I searched high and low, but it's gone. We had it locked away in our fume cupboard along with the other noxious stuff. It should have been sent back. Well, it's not there now, but there seems to be some issue over how it was returned, or if indeed that happened at all.'

Cathy frowned. 'I don't understand. Surely you contact the suppliers and see if it reached them. Then you'll know for sure if the stuff Michael swallowed was from that source. If the stuff they got back had less in it, there you are. He took it from there.'

Saj shook his head. 'Of course, I've tried. It was the first thing I did. I rang them up on Saturday and the police wanted their number as well. I'm hoping the stuff's still in transit. They tell me that they haven't received the returned chemicals at all. Quite off with me, they seemed. The man I spoke to said it wasn't the first time they'd had problems with missing chemicals from our lab. I told him I didn't have a clue what he was talking about. If it's not with them, there's a bottle of very unpleasant stuff floating around somewhere or other, that should really be in a locked cupboard or disposed of safely.'

'Oh, dear...'

They sat in silence for some moments. Cathy knew that this wouldn't look good on the lab and many difficult questions might now have to be answered by both Saj and the professor. 'Who was in charge of sending it back?' she asked. 'Surely they can tell you for certain.'

Saj looked uncomfortable. 'Bit of a mix-up,' he confessed. And then to her raised eyebrows, he sighed again. 'Okay. As it happens, it was your patient, Cathy. It really should have been one of the lab technicians and I'm still to discover how it came about that one of our secretaries was handling dangerous chemicals, but it seems that Sara Wiseman had it. The police are questioning her now.'

17

Sara looked at the ceiling. She saw a stain above and to the right. It looked like coffee. Pale, insipid brown, darker at the edges. If you looked at it from an angle, it took the shape of a dragon, or perhaps it was a man's profile. Sara imagined a difficult interview. An angry exchange. A polystyrene cup tossed skyward.

'Mrs Wiseman?'

She smiled and then, realising how this might look, focused her attention once again on the police detective, a pleasant woman in a suit. She'd been surprised to have a lady police officer interviewing her, but that was quite sexist. Not a mothering sort, Sara had thought as she looked at the woman originally. She was in her late forties also probably, but whereas Sara's hips had spread, the detective was all straight up and down. Had she not had long hair tied back, from behind in her trouser suit she might well have been mistaken for–

'The chemicals, Mrs Wiseman? Can we go through it again?' The woman's voice was cold, expressionless.

Sara swallowed. She had already been asked about the

Sodium-whatever-it-was-called half a dozen times. She cleared her throat. 'I'm not sure...' she began. Perhaps it was better not to expand on what she had said. She'd seen television programmes about this sort of thing. John had gone through a phase of watching them in bed while beside her. She had tried to sleep. Real-crime dramas, or police procedurals, he called them. Lots of shouting and insinuations, and the police were always suspicious of everything and usually corrupt. She looked at the female detective once more and wondered if she had ever misused her power to get the answer she desired. That was surely back in the eighties and even longer ago though. Not nowadays when everything had to be by the book.

The detective sighed. 'I realise it's been a long day. It's vital, you see? The Sodium Azide hasn't arrived at the manufacturers. Can you go through one more time about the courier collection? How late did you stay that Tuesday evening?'

Sara shifted in her seat. Her lower back ached. Why didn't they have comfortable chairs when you were expected to sit for so long? Even her chair at work was more comfortable than this, and she sat at that desk day-in, day-out. Her mind wandered once more. She was back in her office, looking up and through the glass window that separated her and Agnes from the corridor outside. Everyone had to pass the secretaries to get to the pathology lab. She saw him there at the window, his hair slightly tousled in an absent-mindedly beautiful way. His lips, full and pink, parted, revealing an uneven grin. And then the grin suddenly turned to a grimace. He looked at her in a new way. His eyes were narrowed and his teeth bared in a snarl. It was an expression of disgust. Utter contempt.

Sara gasped and clutched at her throat. 'Oh God!' she cried. 'I think I'm...' She was breathing fast. The room seemed to jerk around her. A wave of heat had crept up her. Her chest was tight and a trickle of sweat ran down between her breasts. 'I'm sorry, I can't...' Now the walls darkened and closed in on her. 'I can't breathe,' she heard herself saying and in the distance, someone was saying the words: 'slow down,' again and again.

18

Cathy wasn't sure what to think and in some ways, she was a little disappointed when Saj announced he had paperwork to attend to still and would be leaving them to it following the meal. Suzalinna seemed put out also and chastised him.

'Cathy, you understand, of course?' he asked, smiling slightly. 'I've got a dreadful headache and I need to get some work done. I've already left it too long. I'll be upstairs in my office. Just leave the dishes, I'll see to them when I come down. Sorry to appear rude.'

His eyes were bloodshot with tiredness. Even discussing the upsetting incident seemed to have drained him. Cathy was about to reply when Suzalinna, now happily inebriated having drunk half a bottle of wine alone, answered for her.

'I should think she does mind. You asked her here, after all. You've not answered any of her questions about this mysterious death. If anything, you've caused more confusion. The whole point was to let Cathy hear everything. You've been vague with me when I've asked. Goodness knows why. It's like you don't want us to know. Why the big secret? You know fine well that Cathy is the only person who can look into this if it turns out to be something sinister. Do you really want the police bumbling around your labs unearthing God knows what?'

'Suz,' he said and there was a note of warning in his voice, but she seemed oblivious to it.

'No, Saj, don't "Suz" me. I won't shut up. Listen, suppose this Michael chap didn't top himself. Suppose that. Suicide's bad enough but what if it turns out it was something more? Suppose he was murdered. It could be someone at your work. This secretary of yours perhaps, if she's stolen noxious chemicals from the lab. She must surely be in the frame. What was it you said about the pair of them carrying on? Perhaps they fell out. A lovers' tiff. You know the old saying about a woman scorned? Well? Wouldn't you rather Cathy and I found out about this before the police tear into you? Cathy already has a track record. Discreet, that's what she'd be...'

Cathy had been watching Saj's face. Something that his wife had said had hit a raw nerve and his eyes had changed from apologetic. His mouth was set and his jaw tight. Cathy looked down and saw his fists were clenched. She couldn't remember seeing him that way before, and it frightened her.

Saj stared down at his wife and spoke with a quiet emotionlessness that was far worse than if he had raised his voice. 'Discreet? Perhaps her, but certainly not you. You haven't the first idea about it. Always the first to wade in with an opinion.'

Cathy recoiled in horror. Perhaps he regretted what he had said, particularly with her there to witness it. Saj wasn't the sort to enjoy a 'scene'. It wasn't in his character at all. The room fell silent.

But almost as if someone had flicked a switch, he was

himself again, turning from his wife and smiling at Cathy. 'Sorry for being so rude to you, Cath. It's been a hard couple of days. You'll forgive me, of course?'

She nodded. 'Yes – yes, of course. It's been a strain...'

He moved to the stairs but wasn't done with Suzalinna, who had tutted and was now smiling defiantly at him. Cathy looked across at her friend and willed her to take heed of what her husband had said, but instead, Suzalinna looked up unfeelingly, meeting his gaze.

'You've no idea,' he said to her. 'None at all. It's just a game to you. Someone is dead, do you understand that? A doctor. Someone who was under *my* care.' He left the room, not waiting for an answer. At the top of the stairs, a door banged.

Both women flinched. They sat in silence, but finally, Suzalinna spoke. 'Sorry about that, darling. The last thing you need is us having a bloody domestic in front of you. I did warn you he was in a grump.'

'Oh God, but, Suz,' Cathy said desperately. 'He's upset. You must see it. We can't go making jokes about this man's death, we can't be so frivolous. As he said, it isn't a game, this is real life.'

'He'll come to his senses and apologise later. Anyway, what do you think? Could it be murder then? The more I consider it, the more likely it seems.'

Cathy shook her head. 'Suz, you're not listening. Your husband is in shock and you're still making light of this? He's had enough. You know he hates fuss, and this is about as bad as it can get for him. He's worried about the department and the impact this will have on them. Imagine the indignity of having the place turned over and questions asked about how this man came to die. You've got to leave it. Be sympathetic and give him your support but back off from all of this nonsense now. We're not some Holmes and Watson team. This has to stop.'

Suzalinna seemed to consider what she had said, swilling

the rest of the wine in her glass around and around. 'Have it your way,' she finally said, but Cathy saw her friend's eyes narrow. And to her consternation, almost inaudibly Suzalinna murmured something more: 'I can always do a little digging on my own, I suppose...'

19

When Cathy awoke the following morning, she had a moment of blissful amnesia. The bed was warm and she wrapped the covers more tightly around, enjoying the cocoon of quilt. She stared through half-closed eyes at the ceiling, watching the shadows move. A tree outside cast a pattern and she saw the exaggerated branches distort and nod across her wall. And then it hit her. The previous night. It had been awkward, to say the least. The whole thing had been dreadful. She thought of Suzalinna and Saj. Two friends who she had always envied for their intimacy. Saj, with his infinite patience, his affable calmness. Suzalinna, with her passion and near-arrogance, but unquestionable reliance on her husband's steadying influence. It had been awful to witness them falling out.

Of course, she'd seen them argue before. Suzalinna seemed to enjoy goading her long-suffering husband, forcing him into a response, when he might otherwise rather say nothing. But last night had been different. Admittedly, Suzalinna had been insensitive, but Saj had been so peculiar. Cathy thought of his coldness, the way he had looked at his wife. And then, within a matter of seconds, he had returned to his usual self, turning to Cathy to apologise. Odd, and rather frightening. Why had she never seen that side to him before? Stress had caused it. It was undoubtedly making him overreact. Suzalinna had pushed him too far. Hopefully, after she had left, Suzalinna had had the sense to go upstairs to make amends. Cathy had called up to say goodbye herself, but Saj's door was still firmly closed.

She turned over in her bed and looked at the clock. Five forty-five. She had another fifteen minutes. As she lay there, she considered the problem of Michael Croft's unexpected death. The whole thing was disturbing. Cathy tried to put her thoughts into some kind of order, recalling her strange encounter with Sara Wiseman and the reason she had found out about Michael in the first place. Poor Sara, having just lost her mother, would now need to answer some rather tough questions from the police. But how had the medical secretary come to be mixed up in it? Had she been having an affair with Michael? Did her husband know? She thought of Mr Wiseman then. The tall, rough-looking man in his grubby jeans and T-shirt. He had appeared incredibly concerned for his wife. He'd pulled Cathy aside and spoken to her before she went into the house. She tried to think back over what he had said. Something had rung an alarm bell.

Cathy looked at the clock again, reminded that her own alarm would sound soon. A couple more minutes. But what was it that Mr Wiseman had said? He had told her he was concerned for his wife. Cathy lay there, stupidly trying to force it. And then it came to her. Mr Wiseman had been talking about this wife's reaction on hearing news of the young doctor's death. 'You'd have thought she'd had a hand in it,' he had said. Why on earth had he said that? It was an outrageously insensitive statement to make, even in shock.

'Does her husband believe she was responsible?' Cathy

asked the empty room. Of course, no answer came. But what reason would Sara have to kill Michael? Even if he was her lover, as some rumours suggested, why would she wish him dead? 'The husband. He's got far greater motive,' she said to herself, and then, felt quite sick, because if that was so, Mr Wiseman had deliberately tried to implicate his wife in the crime by mentioning it to Cathy at the start. Had he been trying to deflect attention from himself and onto the woman who had cheated on him? She shook her head, trying to obliterate the thought.

'Anyway,' she told herself. 'Michael Croft wasn't murdered. He left a note.' She smiled at this. 'There was a note.'

With that decided, she got up, throwing the covers off in one swift movement and yelping as the cold air hit her.

'None of your business,' she repeated a couple of times in the shower as the hot water drummed on her head, filling her lungs with steam. But part of her still hadn't settled.

***

She arrived at work early and was surprised to find James's car there already. She knocked on his door before opening her own.

'Didn't expect to see you in before me. I thought I was doing well today,' she said.

Her senior partner leaned back in his chair and sighed. 'Morning, Cathy. You are. We both are but needs must. I'm afraid to say that I didn't get round to all of my lab results last night. I woke up feeling guilty about it and decided that there was no point in lying there, stewing. I was as well coming in and opening up shop. It's good to clear the decks. Glad I did now. Just got a report back about a query melanoma. It turns out that the biopsy was positive. I'll have to ring this morning and break the bad news.'

'How long have you been in?'

'Since seven.'

'Honestly, James. You'll be flagging by three this afternoon! Did you get breakfast?'

'Stop worrying about me. Why are you in early anyway?' He laughed, throwing his pen down on the desk. 'I thought you stayed late the other night as well?'

'Oh, I did. I suppose I was the same as you. Wanted to get a head start, really.'

'All okay?' He looked at her with concern. 'I'm busy but not so completely overrun that I can't see things.'

'James...'

'Come on. Out with it. We've hardly had a chance to catch up these past few weeks, what with patients and meetings. It didn't help that I was away at that COPD conference at the end of last week. So, come on, what's going on?'

Cathy, who had hovered by the door, came into the room.

'Sit,' he ordered, and she did so.

'Same old with work, I suppose,' she said, smiling at him. 'I had a rather odd one the other day though...'

James nodded. 'Go on.'

'A bereavement visit that turned out to be something more. In a way, I'm sort of involved, but from a different angle now. An old medical school friend, her husband...'

James sighed. 'Just start at the beginning.'

'I don't know what to say. I went out to see this woman, Sara Wiseman. Her mother died. Not unexpected. Alzheimer's. Found on the living room floor. I was happy to sign the death certificate, of course, although the police had been called to kick the door down when a neighbour saw the poor dear lying there. No, but that wasn't the issue. When I went to visit Sara, her husband pulled me to one side. He said that she had had a double-whammy that night. Her mother had died, but she had been on a work night out and one of her colleagues was also just found dead. Sara's husband was concerned. He said that she had taken the news of the colleague's death far worse than that of her mother.'

James exhaled. 'Bad luck. But that's not so very strange. The mother had been declining over many months, I presume? This Sara Wiseman had said her goodbyes a long time ago, perhaps. Her mother's death might have been a relief in some ways, although, no doubt she'll have felt guilty for even thinking of it that way.'

Cathy sighed.

'A colleague on the other hand,' James continued. 'That is an entirely different matter, as you well know. A peer, maybe of similar age, that's quite another thing. Unexpected, I assume?'

'It seems that it was suicide.'

'Oh goodness, well no wonder she's cut up. But what did you mean about it being related to your medical school friend? I don't understand.'

'Sara Wiseman is a medical secretary. She works in the pathology labs at the hospital. My friend's husband is a consultant pathologist. He was on the night out with Sara and this other chap who died unexpectedly.'

'Oh, I see. But the police will be looking into it. Why is it playing on your mind so much, Cathy?'

'It shouldn't be, I know. This morning I woke up and made a conscious decision to forget about the whole thing. Of course, my friend's husband is distraught. I had dinner with them last night. He's under a good deal of pressure at the moment. When someone you work with kills themselves and with chemicals from their workplace too... well, questions need to be answered. I worry for him, obviously.'

'So?'

Cathy sighed. 'I know. I know. I'd already decided to let it drop. You're right, of course. You usually are.'

James smiled. 'Sleeping okay, Cathy?'

She nodded. 'I'm fine, honestly, James.'

'When's your next appointment to see your consultant, if you don't mind me asking?'

'Open-ended. I'm just seeing a GP if I have any issues. Really, James, I promise I'm not going off the rails again. It's been a hectic couple of weeks. That's all.'

'You overthink things when you're stressed.'

Cathy laughed. 'So do you, so does everyone. That's nothing to do with the bipolar, that's just human nature.'

'You know I'm here. Even if I'm busy with paperwork and whatever,' he said. 'The door might be closed a lot of the time but metaphorically, it is wide open, okay?'

She nodded and, smiling to herself, went to her room. It was good to talk things through with James. He was the voice of reason when she was more scattered. Cathy switched on the computer and removed her jacket, hanging it on the back of the door. It was chilly, and she rubbed her hands, waiting for the computer to allow her to log in. When it did, she hurried through a few laboratory results and then looked at how her day might pan out. Her morning surgery was almost full, and she had two house visits as well. She looked down the list of names, grimacing as she saw one, a rather complicated patient with multiple complaints that she knew were psychological. And then she looked to her afternoon slots. A few were taken but many were still empty; that was good. She noticed her final patient for the day and her heart sank. Not someone she had expected to see at all. John Wiseman. Why might he want to see her again so soon? Perhaps it wouldn't be so easy to forget this dreadful affair as she had hoped.

20

'I'll be straight with you. I'm not happy.'

Anxiety sat in the pit of Cathy's stomach until the time came. 'Mr Wiseman? Please, if I can help at all? You collected your mother-in-law's death certificate from the front desk, I believe? The receptionist told me.'

The man shifted in his seat. He had entered the room in a forceful and morose manner, flopping himself down in the seat opposite her without a word. Now it seemed he had plenty to get off his chest.

'It's not the death certificate. That's fine. Well, dear God, I hope it's fine. I assume you still stand by what you wrote?'

Cathy's eyes widened. 'Yes. Of course. Why might you think otherwise?'

He shook his head. 'No, it doesn't matter. I wondered, that's all. Can I ask instead about my wife? I think you knew very well when you came out to see her, didn't you? I said a little to you at the door, but I got the impression that you saw something when you spoke with her? You saw something strange in her behaviour too? The police have been asking questions. She was so flustered, she had a panic attack in the station and had to be taken home in a police car. Goodness knows what the neighbours are thinking. Believe me, I feel bad enough saying this. I'm her husband, for God's sake. Traitor, more like now.'

Cathy shook her head in confusion. 'No. I'm sorry Mr Wiseman, I don't understand.' Was he really trying in some way to implicate his wife in the death of Michael Croft? The idea made her distinctly uneasy. 'Your wife had a shock,' she went on. 'I hope that she's doing better. I'm unsure what made you think that I had perceived something else. As far as I was concerned, she was having a natural grief reaction to a dreadful set of circumstances. Grief can hit people in different ways. I thought she behaved appropriately. How is she, can I ask?'

He sighed and looked past her and out of the window to the playing fields that lay beyond the practice car park. The neighbouring school was using them and Cathy could hear the muffled shouts of children enjoying the fresh air. 'Not great,' he answered. 'Hardly talking to me now. The police were asking her questions all yesterday. She came home exhausted. She should be planning her mother's funeral, but she told me this morning that I'm to speak to the undertakers myself. A quick, simple service was all she would say. Honestly, I don't know what to think. I know she's been having some kind of mid-life crisis these past few months. I think we fell into a bit of a rut. You know how it is? I've been busy with work.'

'What is it you do, Mr Wiseman?'

'I run the building site up the road. Glainkirk Homes. We're building up by the roundabout. It's been busy enough. One of my lads had an accident the other week so we're a man down. I've taken the week off because of all this. Couldn't have happened at a worse time. I suppose I've been letting Sara get on with her own thing while I've been working. She always seemed happy enough going into the hospital and so on. I never really noticed. I suppose her mother, and the strain of all of that, must have taken its toll; sent her into a breakdown of some sort. I thought having her next to us had made it easier. She was essentially at the bottom of the garden. All Sara had to do was cross the lawn to get to the gate. She took her mother's breakfast over in the morning and did evening meals, tucked her in for the night. I thought it was what Sara wanted. She'd always said her mother didn't want to go into a home. That's why I built the granny flat in the first place. It was meant to be easier,' he repeated.

'Why do you think your wife has had a breakdown?' Cathy asked.

'The night this all kicked off. It was before she even headed out. She was cold with me. Emotionless. I've never seen her that way before. She went over to her mother's house like she was in a trance. Told me to pick her up at the door. She said she didn't want to come back to the house, that I was to be waiting at her mother's gate. She was strange. I asked how her mother was when she got in the car and she wouldn't talk. We drove to the restaurant in silence. I knew she must have been angry with me. We had a bit of a fall-out earlier when she was getting dressed. I wasn't so keen on her going out at all. Couldn't see the point of it.' He shifted in his seat again. 'She moaned about the folk she worked with, and I didn't understand why she'd want to spend the evening with them. I was a bit childish. I told her I might go out drinking too that night. I didn't, of course. I went right home and waited for her to phone. And then, I got a call from her. It must have been before ten. She sounded awful. Wanted me to collect her right away. She was on the verge of tears. I assumed the night hadn't gone well, or she was feeling guilty for being so off with me earlier. I drove straight there to collect her. The rest of them were going clubbing, it seems.'

'But why was she so upset? Did she say? By that point, her

colleague was surely still alive, and as far as she knew, her mother was safely tucked up in bed.'

'Yes, I know. That's what's worrying me now. She shouldn't have been so upset then. She got in the car and I could see she was shaking. I drove. I knew she wanted to tell me something...'

Cathy watched Mr Wiseman. His face looked pained.

'I wondered if she had been having an affair. There, that's what it is.'

Cathy nodded. The rumours about Sara and Michael Croft might well have had more substance to them than Saj had thought.

'Did she manage to talk to you in the car?'

'I took her to our old house, where we used to live years ago. I don't know why I did. Maybe to show her that nothing had changed between us. That I was still the man she married. Since we moved, it feels like everything changed. The fun left us. The kids moved out and her mother moved in next door. I suppose to her, it must have felt like a trap or something. She tried to explain in the car. Maybe I should have let her then. She won't speak at all now.'

'What did she want to say?'

'I thought she wanted to confess to an affair, but now I wonder...'

Cathy waited, barely daring to breathe. In the end, it came. He looked directly at her. His eyes were wide and alarmed.

'I'm worried now. I'm afraid that she's done something.' He ran a hand across his forehead. He had gone quite pale. 'I'm scared she's done something she shouldn't. It seems odd. Two people dying like that. The police have been asking questions. They pulled me to one side and asked if I'd seen anything. A tub of some chemical or other has gone missing, apparently. It's what this colleague of hers has supposedly taken to kill himself. Now, I'm panicking.'

Cathy still didn't understand, and she shook her head.

'I'm not explaining right, I know,' he agreed. 'There was something strange when she got in the car from seeing her mum that night. It's been playing on my mind since the police spoke to me. Goodness knows what she told them. She'd been monosyllabic with me ever since. I don't even know if she's under suspicion now. Perhaps I should have said something myself to them, but it only occurred to me after they left, and how could I do that to her? Dob my own wife in. It isn't right.' He looked at Cathy with an air of desperation and then, deciding, he went on. 'I don't know if I'm right telling you this. I don't know what to do for the best.' He shook his head and grimaced. Cathy wondered what was coming. 'Before she went out for the evening, her jacket hit against the door and made an odd noise. I asked her what she had in her pocket. She didn't say. But if looks could kill, I'd have been lying in the morgue alongside that Michael chap and her mother now.'

21

'I've got news!' Suzalinna hissed. 'Honestly, you won't believe what I have to tell you!'

'Why are you whispering?' Cathy asked.

She had arrived home from work, having failed to resolve the issue over Mrs Wiseman. She'd promised her husband to look into it but in truth, had no idea where to begin. The thought of calling the police and suggesting Sara's mother might have died of anything other than natural causes filled her with dread, especially given how happily she had signed off the death certificate. Better to think it over calmly, she told herself as she locked her consulting room door for the night. She hadn't had a chance to catch James, but then, what would she have told him? The whole thing was very disturbing but she knew James was already concerned for her and she didn't want him worried even more.

'I'm speaking quietly, not whispering,' Suzalinna said. 'Saj is in the next room, and he won't approve. But what he doesn't know, won't hurt him. It's for his own good I'm doing it, anyway.'

Cathy's heart sank. 'I hope you two are talking? What's going on? Is Saj all right?'

Her friend tutted. 'Silly. Of course, we're both all right. Saj just wanted to have a little sulk. He doesn't need to be worrying about this. Like I told you, I'm looking into it for him.'

'Suz, you know you can't do that.'

'Who says? You're not the only one who can do this investigating stuff. I bet I've found out a good deal more than you have already. I'm just being kind in sharing my findings with you. I thought we could do an information swap. I'll tell you mine if you tell me yours. What do you think?'

'I don't think you're taking this seriously.'

'I doubt you'll say that when you hear what I have to tell you. I must say, you're being horribly stiff about it. I told you before, this is my chance to do something out of the ordinary. Imagine how proud Saj will be if I get to the bottom of things. I assume you've jumped to the same conclusion as me – that it was murder?'

Cathy nearly choked. 'No, I have not!'

Suzalinna tutted. 'You're losing your touch then, aren't you? Do you want to hear my news, or are you going to be a sourpuss?'

Cathy sighed and moved the phone to her other ear. She had been looking out of the kitchen window, but she turned and made her way through to the living room, flopping down on her sofa and folding her legs under her. 'Go on then. Hit me with it, Sherlock.'

Suzalinna giggled. 'Well, I've done a bit of digging. I know a couple of these people, remember? I've been on work nights out with Saj in the past, so it's not been as difficult as you might think. I'll admit, I had to borrow his mobile, just to get a couple of numbers and to read a few text messages...'

'Suzalinna!'

'Yes, I know, but it was for a good cause, and he'll understand. Saj has nothing to hide, anyway. He's far too busy with work. So, now that we're past that little shock, let me tell you what I heard from Jennifer.'

'Jennifer?'

'Lab technician. Not the most senior, that's Hughie, and he's a bundle of laughs – not. Last time I sat next to him at a departmental meal, he bent my ear for a good hour telling me how criminal it was that they paid the lab technicians barely half that of junior doctors when they did far more important work. He's a horrible ginger-haired, weaselly guy. Stubborn eyebrows and thick chin.'

Cathy laughed at the description.

'Three techies work in the department,' Suzalinna continued. 'Ettie, Hughie and Jennifer. They prepare the slides and whatnot for the doctors. I think they do some of the simple reporting too.'

'And there are three doctors?'

'Well, two now, darling, but yes. Michael, Saj and old Professor Huxley.'

'So, what was this Jennifer-girl saying? She must have thought it a bit odd you phoning her up out of the blue?'

'I told a white lie, as it happens. I said that Saj had been worried about the technicians after what had happened. I told her he was caught up talking with the police. Which to be fair, was true yesterday. They had him in for another grilling, along with that secretary woman, so it seems. Anyway,' Suzalinna sighed, 'I said that he had asked me to ring round and check that they were all okay. The department's still shut for the time being so it wasn't so odd me asking. I spun her an excuse of being an emergency consultant and being used to dealing with trauma, blah, blah, you know the kind of waffle.'

'But Saj will find out you've interfered as soon as he speaks to them at work.' Cathy absently picked up the cushion beside her and pummelled it into shape.

'Oh, I know that, but I'll tell him something or other. I told you before, this is for his own good. I'm beginning to think that the police suspect him, what with the amount of time they're spending quizzing him about the ins and outs of the lab.'

'I hope you're wrong.'

'So do I. Now, are you going to let me speak?'

Cathy snorted. 'Hurry up then.'

'Well,' Suzalinna said, but her voice became distant. The phone crackled loudly making Cathy jump and move it away from her ear. 'Sorry,' Suzalinna said. 'I was just shutting the door properly. Right, it seems that this Michael lad had a few little things going on. For one, he was a drug user!'

'Really?' Cathy was unable to hide her incredulity. 'What, in a big way?'

'Well, from what Jennifer said, he had been using the whole time he was working there. Diazepam, apparently.'

'Street?'

'So it seems. I doubt he was sidling up to some dealer at the back of a pub car park, but he wasn't stealing it from the hospital, as far as I know. These people always find a way to get it. I don't know why he started or when, but it was an established habit.'

'How did she know?'

'Saw him with the stuff, apparently.'

'Points towards suicide then...'

'Why do you say that? Debt? Depression? That sort of thing, you think?'

'Well, I guess so.'

'I disagree, darling. Quite the opposite. What if it emerged that he was abusing drugs, especially when he was on call for the lab? If that came out, he'd be in really serious trouble. Blackmail, Cathy! What if someone in the lab knew about his little habit? Chances are, a good few of them did, if this Jennifer-girl was so sure of it. Well then, what if they were blackmailing him?'

'Suz, it's the wrong way about. Michael would have a motive to kill his blackmailer, not the other way around. Blackmailers certainly don't want to kill off their income. Really, I thought you had more than this.' She shifted on the sofa. Her feet were bare, and she stretched them out and inspected her toes, wiggling them.

Suzalinna sighed. 'I suppose that is true. Okay, how about this: Michael threatens his blackmailer that he'll go to the top and tell the professor that he's being pumped for money. Michael might well get his knuckles rapped for using drugs, but chances are, he'd be given support to get off the stuff and a simple warning from the deanery. He wouldn't lose his career over a bit of vallie.'

Cathy flopped back again. 'Vallie? God, Suz.'

'You see and hear it all in A&E. Well, what do you think? The blackmailer wouldn't get off so lightly, perhaps. Michael goes to rehab and the money-grabbing crook gets the sack. Michael's character is not as clean as we might have first thought, anyway. When suicide was mentioned, I suppose people assumed he was a hard-worked perfectionistic sort, who found the stress of dealing with death in the path lab too much. It doesn't look like that now though, does it?'

'I don't think we believed he was squeaky-clean at all though,' Cathy said. 'We'd already heard that he might be having an affair with one of the secretaries. Even Saj knew that and he's probably the last to know about these sorts of things.'

'I wonder if his wife knew,' Suzalinna said meditatively.

'Suz, I don't want to spoil your fun, but none of this really matters, does it? They found a note. The police are convinced it was a straightforward suicide. It had to be. He did it with chemicals from the lab. I know someone might get into trouble for leaving the poisonous stuff lying around, but Michael did it. He took the stuff himself. We've no evidence that anyone forced him.'

'Suicide? On a night out with his work colleagues? I'm not falling for that. You know as well as I do, that people don't do it that way. I don't care what this note said. It has to be an odd bit of paper that the murderer's found with Michael's handwriting on it. They've taken advantage of their little find. It'll say something like: 'So sorry, I can't keep going on like this...' and a bit at the end will be torn off. In fact, Michael will have been writing to his supervisor about changing from the pathology rotation, or something of the kind. The murderer will have pocketed the paper to use later, hoping we'd all fall for the suicide ploy. This happens all the time in TV dramas.'

'It's not quite right...' Cathy began, but Suzalinna wasn't having any of it and was more than a little disappointed when she admitted she hadn't looked into the case at all herself.

'Anyone would think you weren't interested in the thing,' Suzalinna said, huffily. 'I'm beavering away and you give me nothing back.'

In truth, Cathy had more than enough on her mind, worrying about what she should do the following day. She had already decided that she couldn't allow Mr Wiseman's allegation about his wife to go unreported. That meant a difficult conversation with the police...

'Well, I'll speak to you another time when you're more attentive,' Suzalinna concluded. 'By then, I'll have probably solved the whole thing myself.'

Cathy knew that nothing she could say would alter her friend's resolve. She just hoped that it wouldn't land herself or Saj in any trouble.

22

'I'm sorry to call first thing when no doubt you're very busy,' Cathy said.

She had to do it then. She couldn't have waited a moment longer. She'd barely slept for thinking about it all night. What on earth would Suzalinna have said if she had told her the evening before?

'What is it I can do for you, doctor?' the inspector asked.

'It's a rather delicate matter,' she admitted, wishing her heart wasn't hammering so loudly in her ears. She'd planned how she was going to word it, over and over in her head all the previous night, but now, her mouth was dry and she found that she had forgotten everything she wanted to say. 'I– Well, as I say, it's a little awkward. I've heard that you have been speaking with Mrs Sara Wiseman about her involvement in... Well, not involvement perhaps, I mean, her position as a secretary at the hospital pathology labs. I'm her GP and I went out to see her. I was doing a bereavement visit after her mother passed away. I'm sure you have rules, as we do, about confidentiality and you'll not want to tell me anything, but I think you've been enquiring about the chemicals that seem to have gone missing from the lab just before this young doctor died?' Cathy paused, trying to gather her thoughts. 'I'm sorry. It's not quite coming out right.'

The police inspector, who she knew quite well, sighed but didn't speak.

'I know. I'm sorry,' she repeated. 'I sound as if I'm interfering, and really, I'm not. It's just I'm wondering if perhaps we should have requested a post-mortem for Sara Wiseman's mother, after all.'

She heard the man at the end of the line clear his throat. 'Dr Moreland,' he said. 'Let me get this straight. You are now having doubts about the circumstances of another death, one that you, I seem to remember, were only too happy to sign off? Can I ask why the sudden change of heart and what on earth this has to do with the other man's death?'

Cathy took a deep breath. It wasn't going as she had intended. 'As you know, I can't breach confidentiality,' she said. 'But someone has hinted to me that there is a suspicion now about Mrs Wiseman being involved in her mother's death. I realise that it's hearsay, really I do, but if she had access to toxic chemicals from the pathology lab where she worked, might she have used a lethal dose on her mother? I assume it was some sort of mercy killing. I'm not suggesting it was for any gain otherwise.'

He was sceptical. 'So, you called me to say that?'

'Isn't that enough?'

He sighed heavily again. Cathy knew she sounded hysterical. She shouldn't have said 'hinted' and 'hearsay.' That had made it much worse. She looked like a gossip now.

'Doctor, I have personally spoken with both Mr and Mrs Wiseman myself. I did so yesterday after Mrs Wiseman had been formally questioned by my colleague. I can't go into details with you, as I'm sure you'll appreciate. At the moment, Mrs

Wiseman is still helping us with our investigations into the tragic suicide of one of her colleagues. That, and the death of her poor mother, are not, as far as I am concerned, up for debate. Certainly, not with outsiders. I've read the report about her mother. Two very experienced police officers attended the scene, along with the ambulance service. Not one of them raised a concern about the old lady's death. You, yourself, were happy to complete the death certificate. I can set your mind at rest now. I have no concerns myself about this. You have already helped the police out a good deal in the past. I appreciate that. But in this case, I will have to put my foot down. It's been done. The certificate is signed. I assume that the funeral hasn't yet taken place? I really think that the Wisemans have had enough to deal with without some gossip's take on the thing.'

'You must realise that I wouldn't phone you if I wasn't concerned. I'd never usually suggest a post-mortem after issuing a death certificate already. Certainly not unless I was genuinely worried, and I am. I realise it reflects terribly on my reputation to even make this telephone call. I couldn't leave it though.'

The police inspector coughed. 'If you'll excuse me for saying so, doctor, I'm far less concerned about your reputation than I am for the safeguarding of my colleagues and their resources. Wasting police time, not to mention that of the police surgeon...'

Cathy had lost him. 'It's fine,' she said. 'Thank you for listening.' What a mess she'd made of it. And what a fool she had sounded. She could just imagine him hanging up and turning to the officer sitting beside him. 'Bloody interfering cow,' he'd have said. And he'd have been right too. Cathy knew she was meddling. It would be far simpler for everyone if she told Mr Wiseman that she had spoken to the police and they, and she, were now completely satisfied with his mother-in-law's cause of death.

She rested back in her chair. Her head ached. What on earth

was she going to do? If Mr Wiseman was right, how could she live with herself? An old lady might have died before her time. Cathy knew the cruelty of Alzheimer's disease, having witnessed many patients, along with her own grandmother, suffer its effects. She could even understand Mrs Wiseman's motives for considering it if she had. Watching someone you love lose all sense of self, was appalling. But euthanasia was illegal. She remembered her district nurse's words from only a few days back, when she told Cathy that Mrs Wiseman had spoken with her about the subject. Was it possible that she had decided to go through with it herself?

There was a knock at the door, and without waiting for an answer, it opened. James's head appeared. 'Thought I heard you on the phone sounding a bit irate. All okay?'

Cathy sighed.

'Clearly not,' her partner said.

'Police,' she told him, not wanting to explain.

'Oh?' James asked and came further into the room. 'I know we're both about to start for the day, but do you want to talk?'

'Honestly?' Cathy smiled unhappily. 'James, please don't go on at me. Not now. I can't stand a big heart-to-heart.'

'Get through the morning and we'll chat over coffee.'

'Thanks, James, but I don't need this. I wish you'd leave it. I'm stretched as it is without chats over coffee. Rest assured, I'm not having a breakdown. I've told you that already.'

When he left, she knew that she'd spoken out of turn. But she needed to focus on her work. She was fully booked and had already seen that her first two patients were going to be tricky. The results of a referral that hadn't been favourable, and a chronic pain issue.

'If only Mr Wiseman hadn't said anything,' she said to herself. 'And why confide in me anyway? Why not ask his wife?'

The Wisemans were undoubtedly an odd pair. But as Cathy began her surgery, she knew in her heart she couldn't let the thing rest. Before heading out on visits, she'd make a further telephone call. This time, to the procurator fiscal.

23

'Cathy? Is now a good time?'

'Saj, how are you? I didn't expect you to call.'

He laughed. 'Back to work today and the first PM I'm asked to do is one of yours. I had to call, of course. The fiscal says that you're concerned? What is it you want me to look for then?'

Cathy had made the difficult phone call earlier. They hadn't been shocked or upset by her request to hold the death certificate and ask for a routine post-mortem.

'It's not commonplace,' the fiscal admitted. 'But certainly not unheard of if families are in dispute with the doctor about the cause of death.'

Cathy hadn't said that one family member had near-enough accused another of murder, but she had been glad when it was agreed.

'I'll contact the hospital mortuary,' the fiscal had promised. 'Can I leave the family to you?'

Cathy had dreaded that conversation more than any other, but as it turned out, Sara Wiseman was almost disinterested when she told her about the delay in the funeral.

'If it has to be done...' she had said.

Cathy was surprised, but also relieved. It meant the woman was likely to be innocent.

Now at home, having made the necessary calls and finished her work for the day, she had been just about to phone James. She had been rude to him earlier and had avoided any conversation with him since in case he rebuked her for interfering in police business instead of getting on with her busy-enough job.

But Saj was speaking. 'Cathy?'

'Sorry, yes. I assume you know it's your secretary's mother? I didn't think it would be you doing the PM, to be honest. It's very late to be starting anyway, isn't it?'

'Yes, I know. We've been busy. Sara's off on compassionate leave. Otherwise, the nearest hospital would have taken the case. I hear the police weren't interested, so we're obviously not thinking about foul play. You put stroke on the original certificate. Will I just open her up, have a root about and see what I can find?'

Cathy grimaced. 'You have to remember; I'm not used to this kind of talk.'

Saj laughed. 'Sorry. Force of habit. That was insensitive. It's been a long day already, catching up with work. The labs have been non-stop. Obviously, the office is bad too because Sara's not here. All in all, not a great day. Anyway, back to your concerns over this one...'

'I just wanted a concrete cause of death for the family. I had a feeling that it might not be a straightforward stroke, after all. I'd hate to have missed something and made a mistake on the form. I wondered about the old lady's stomach contents...'

'So, you are thinking foul play? You know I shouldn't be doing this then. We only do routines, not suspicious deaths.'

Cathy sighed. 'I'm at my wit's end. I've already spoken to the police today. They're not interested. Please. Just to satisfy my curiosity...'

'You sound like Suzalinna,' he said. 'All right. I'm only doing it as it's you. I'll start work now. Hopefully, by tomorrow...'

'Saj?'

'What?' He sounded tired.

'Thanks. I mean it. Before you go, how are you coping? I assume the rest of the team are back at it? Is it a lot more work for everyone now that you're a man down?'

He laughed. 'Like Hughie was saying earlier to me, Michael was often more trouble than he was a help. We've been trying to get through as best we can, thanks. The lab technicians are always stretched, though. One of the secretaries went to visit Michael's wife, or rather widow, the other night. She's still in shock, of course. But then, life in the hospital must go on. The prof is fuming because his research project has stalled. He was doing a paper with Michael and I think he was counting on the help. The techies are struggling because, although Michael was a nuisance at times, he was an extra pair of hands, or eyes, at a microscope.'

'Have you heard anything more from the police? I assume the missing chemicals haven't turned up again?'

Saj groaned. 'No to both. The police seem to have left us in peace for the time being. They must be satisfied to put his death down as a suicide. There will be questions about his reason to do such a thing, of course.'

'Do you know what Michael said in the note?'

'Very little, it seems. It was in his wallet. It must have fallen out of his jacket when he got home. The neighbour only spotted it in the garden the following morning.'

'Did he give a reason then?'

'Just that he couldn't go on like this. He was living a lie or something of the kind.'

'Vague, but it seems to eliminate Suzalinna's assumption.'

'Oh?'

'I'm surprised she's not bent your ear yet. I thought she'd have been full of it at home. She rang me up and had all kinds of suggestions about who might have been involved. She'd spoken to at least one of your lab technicians and had even heard that Michael had a bit of a habit.'

'What, drugs?'

'That's what she said. Who knows? It's probably just gossip. And anyway, it wouldn't be so unexpected. Half the junior doctors seem to be high on something or other by the sounds of things now. I was reading about it the other day. It doesn't change the fact that Michael ended things. No one else was involved.'

'Why would anyone be involved? Isn't suicide tragic enough? I really can't understand this obsession with murder. As a rule, people don't get killed. I know you've had your unfortunate brushes with death, Cathy, but generally...'

She laughed. 'You know only too well that Suzalinna's determined to have her murder. She's bored, Saj. You two are okay, aren't you? Things were strained the other night.'

He didn't speak for a moment. 'Fine. Yes.'

'Listen, I hope I haven't put my foot in it, saying what I have? I thought Suz would have spoken to you by now.'

'It's fine, Cathy. Listen, I'd better crack on.'

'Sure. I'll speak to you later. Thanks for doing this for me. I appreciate it, really.'

When she hung up, she felt she had indeed put her foot in it. If things had been tense between the husband and wife, they might only be more so now that she had blabbed. And, of course, it didn't take a brain surgeon to work out where Suzalinna had got his lab technician's details from. Saj would be furious, and rightly so, knowing that his wife had gone through his phone.

'Oh, God.' Cathy sighed. 'I've been an idiot.'

It was gone six o'clock. She knew poor Saj would be working at the lab at least for another couple of hours now. Impulsively, she snatched up her mobile again and rang her friend. There was no answer. Damn it. She'd have liked at least to have forewarned Suzalinna that she'd said the wrong thing and Saj might come home angry.

Instead, she called James and apologised for being brusque earlier. It seemed that she'd caused quite enough trouble for one day.

'It's fine,' James said. 'I could see you weren't in the mood for a big heart-to-heart. I was having a bad one myself.'

'Oh?' Cathy asked. 'Anything I can help with?'

'No, nothing. I think I'll receive a complaint though and you might well have to mediate. Unfair, as it was completely out of my hands too, but anyway... Go to bed early, Cathy, and know that I'm not angry with you. Tomorrow's a new day for both of us.'

24

The street was thankfully quiet. Sara had parked her car on the far side, not knowing why she was there at all, but feeling that she must come. Switching the engine off, she waited. John hadn't woken when she left, creeping out just as dawn broke. He was so used to her routine of getting up early to see to her mother that it probably hadn't even pierced his subconscious.

He had been on her mind constantly. The nights she had lain beside John, the quilt heavy on her legs. In her head, she had been light-footed and supple, dancing in Michael's arms, smiling into his eyes. Never had a person filled her thoughts so consistently. Never had she longed for someone so deeply.

Up until that morning, she had not allowed herself to think of the night of Michael's death. Even when the police questioned her, she would only skim the edge, not allowing her consciousness to touch the side. If she did, she'd have fallen in and never pulled herself out of the gloomy water. The meal had been so traumatic. To reflect on it was almost too much for her to bear. But as things had filtered through to her via John, she had pieced together parts of what had happened.

She allowed her thoughts to linger on that terrible evening. It had begun before she even left her mother's house. In fact, the chain of events had started long before then. That bloody chemical. It had been put in her way by some higher devilment. If she had believed in God, she might have cursed him for allowing such temptation. The draw had been so great. It had been so easy, too easy.

She pulled down the visor now that the sun had risen further. The house at the end of the street was silent, the blinds drawn. How did Victoria really feel? If Michael's wife had loved him as much as her, she would be unable to sleep, unable to do anything. But Sara had a feeling that it wasn't like that. Victoria was young and she'd no doubt remarry. She'd have people around her, doting parents perhaps. Maybe they were staying with her now.

Sara thought of her own parents, her father long since dead, and what of her mother? She thought back to that last evening. She couldn't remember exactly what her mother had said. She supposed it was self-preservation, blocking it out now. Most of her recent memories were a blur. She had been difficult that night and Sara had known she was short on time. She had told John to meet her outside in the car. But her mother hadn't wanted her to leave. She shouldn't have worn her going-out clothes to the house. It had only confused her mother further. That night had seemed like a culmination of so many endings.

John had been impatient outside. She had heard him tooting his horn to hurry her along. She had panicked.

'Mum, let go of me,' she had said and tugged her arm free of the old woman.

She had the bottle ready in her hand. The milky drink to settle her mother for the evening was by her bedside.

And yet, at the last minute, she had wondered if it was the right thing.

Perhaps her mother had held her gaze for too long. Her watery eyes had held a fragment of something, possibly recognition, for a moment. She blamed John for that. If she hadn't been rushed... But there it was. Sara was haunted by images of her mother lying confused and frightened. Perhaps they would stay with her forever.

Sara shifted in her seat. Her leg had cramped. She hadn't taken her eyes off the house since she had arrived. He had lain there, died there. There, on that doorstep, with only his undeserving wife to comfort him. Had hers been the last face he saw? Had her words been the last sound he heard? Sara couldn't bear it.

One of the blinds at the window shifted and was then suddenly drawn. Sara slouched lower in her seat and hoped she hadn't been spotted. At the upstairs window, a woman in a pale nightgown looked out. From the distance she was at, Sara couldn't make out her features, but her hair, dark and long, flowed over her shoulders. The woman stretched and reaching behind, scooped the strands off her neck, holding them high. Not the action of a grieving widow. Sara wondered for the first time if she had another man in the house already. Only one car was parked in the drive, but the street had many others. Had Victoria been waiting for her husband's death? Had she been ready to move someone else in to replace Michael so soon? Sara grimaced. It made her feel quite sick.

The woman at the window turned. Sara thought she looked like she was smiling. She started the car, unable to assimilate this new trajectory of thought. Of course, Victoria had been in many ways responsible for his death. Had she not been such a cold wife, and Sara now felt sure that she must have been, he might still be alive today. Victoria had warped his character, made him cruel as she was. Yes. It all made sense.

25

'You tried to call?'

'I did,' Cathy admitted the following morning. 'But I'm surprised that you're even talking to me.'

'Because of Saj?' Suzalinna asked. 'Honestly, that's the last thing I'm thinking about. Let him have his bit of fun sleeping in the spare room for all I care.'

'Oh, Suz, he's not.'

'He is. Came home after eleven last night and set up camp there. Said I had invaded his privacy. I thought after being married for nearly seven years, we didn't need any privacy. Honestly. He can be such a child at times. All I did was look at his phone.'

'I'm worried.'

'About us? Don't be. It'll pass. Now, have you got any news for me?'

Cathy sighed. 'I called last night to warn you I had put my foot in it with Saj earlier, that was all.'

'Why were you talking to him, anyway?' Suzalinna asked. 'He wouldn't explain anything, just went to bed in a huff.'

'Oh, he was doing a post-mortem for me.'

'Really? So, you're now requesting personal dissections, are you? Come out, spit it. Why was he involved? You know it never works that way.'

'As it happens, it was Sara Wiseman's mother. I put stroke on the death certificate but I had a niggle.'

'Did you really, Cathy Moreland? And why might that be? I don't suppose it's because Sara is your number one suspect for another death that night and you think she might just be a double murderer?'

'When you say it like that, it sounds absurd.'

'But that's what you're thinking, isn't it? Sara's been on my mind, too. She has a motive for sure. I heard that there was a good deal of flirting going on during the meal that night. She and Michael were carrying on as if they were a pair of silly teenagers and certainly didn't seem to remember that they had both made their marriage vows to other people.'

'Why would she kill him then?' Cathy asked, despising herself for even falling in line with this conversation.

'Something odd happened that night. There was a bit of coming and going at the table. A few of them got up to go to the loo, and they were having the buffet, so there was that too. It seems that Michael left the table to take a telephone call. Sara went missing for a bit around the same time. When she did come back, something had changed.'

'What?' Cathy asked, unable to help herself.

'Difficult to say. Ettie was puzzled herself. But the mood had altered.'

'Oh, so Ettie was your source? You've pumped Jennifer already and moved on to her?'

'What else could I do? Saj won't have noticed a bloody thing at that meal and anyway, he's not talking to me.'

'He told me that one of the secretaries had been to visit Michael's widow.'

'Oh, I know that, darling. Sorry to steal your thunder. I'd like to visit the lovely Victoria myself, but I can't think of the best route in...'

'Suz, please don't. It's totally inappropriate. I can just about accept you speaking to Saj's colleagues, but as for going to Michael's widow, a woman you've never even met, well, it would be really bad.'

Her friend sighed. 'You don't need to lecture me, Cathy. I'm not completely without tact, you know? But I have other lines of enquiry, anyway.'

'Oh? I assume you're now working your way around the others? Who's left? Hughie, the professor?'

'You're forgetting someone.'

Cathy waited.

'Agnes!' Suzalinna exploded.

'The other medical secretary?'

'Yes. She slipped under the radar, I think, because she seemed above suspicion being quite old. But someone put something in Michael's food or drink that night, I'm sure of it. They all had an opportunity. I just need to pinpoint the motive. I'm seeing Agnes this evening for a little chat after I finish up with something else. Fancy tagging along and keeping me company? I know you're as interested to hear about this Sara Wiseman as I am. Who better to dish the dirt, than the very woman who works right alongside her every day?'

―――――――

It was seven-fifteen and, as agreed, Cathy waited outside the newsagents in the hospital foyer. She had no idea why the meeting had to take place here. Perhaps it was the only place Agnes felt comfortable. Certainly, sitting in a seedy pub on the high street didn't seem appropriate, so it was maybe just as well.

The hospital was still quite busy but visiting hours would soon be over and the relatives and friends who had entered the wards carrying books, cards and provisions for their loved ones, would exit, swarming up the stone steps to the car parks.

As she waited, Cathy thought of her medical school days. It was in this hospital that she had trained. She recalled the scrum in the corridor leading to the lecture theatres and the funny hidden door that led to the clinical skills unit where they learned their trade. A good deal of her education had happened on the wards, too. The patients knew that being unwell in a teaching hospital often meant a medical student sidling up to their bed, hoping for an interview. Cathy smiled as she recalled her first faltering attempts to take a history, to do a medical examination and then to take blood. All small milestones for her and her peers alike, as they slowly gathered confidence and knowledge. Some of the senior doctors who had taught them on the wards had been quite inspiring; others had not. Cathy remembered one professor regularly hurling patient case notes at the final year students if they got a question wrong on his grand ward rounds.

She was inwardly cringing as she remembered one of her incorrect answers when someone tapped her on the shoulder. She turned, expecting to see Suzalinna.

'Cathy bloody-Moreland! I knew it was you!'

It was not her friend, but another familiar face.

'My God!' She laughed, stepping back. 'I had no idea, Chris. It's been a while; how funny to see you here.'

He grinned. 'I only came back six weeks ago. I didn't realise you'd stuck around.'

Cathy shook her head in disbelief. 'I was just thinking about the grand ward rounds. Do you remember?'

He laughed. 'Goodness, don't. I have nightmares about them

still. Feels like a lifetime ago now. So, what are you doing then, Cathy? Weren't you headed for GP Land?'

'Yes. I'm a partner. I'm hanging around waiting for Suzalinna. Remember her?'

'How could anyone from our year forget Suzalinna? She's A&E though, isn't she? I've seen her in the corridor in passing, but she didn't recognise me or was too busy. You stuck close by then. Didn't fancy travelling?'

'My practice is just down the road. No, I'm a home bird. You were going to Australia, weren't you? You had a surgical rotation there. Hadn't you made a connection after doing your elective? Where are you now?'

He was nodding.

'Sorry.' She laughed. 'So many questions. It is good to see you.'

They both grinned at one another.

'I settled on plastics in the end.'

'No way!'

'Yes, but NHS, not private. Australia was great, but I suppose I got homesick. I had a relationship break down and thought, well, nothing was keeping me there anymore, so I started planning a transfer back to Scotland. I've just finished a shift, as it happens. I'd suggest a coffee but I'm done in. Need to go home and get to bed. We should meet up some time, though. Bit of a medical school reunion?'

Cathy laughed. 'I've had enough of them to last me a lifetime.' And then to his puzzled expression, she said, 'Ignore me. You missed the last one because you were abroad. You know how they go.'

'I can imagine. Yes. Everyone keen to exaggerate?'

'Some. Others were lovely to catch up with. Listen, I'll let you go.' All the while, he had been fiddling with his car keys.

'Let's swap numbers. It's a pity Suz is running late. I'm sure she'd have enjoyed seeing you too.'

He had already pulled out his mobile and typed in her name. 'Shoot,' he said, and she told him. 'Okay, Cathy Moreland. Good to see you,' he said. 'Brightened up an otherwise dismal shift.'

'Bad one?' she asked as he walked back towards the door.

'House fire, nasty,' he answered, and she grimaced. 'Anyway. I'll be in touch. Promise.'

When he left, she smiled for some time, despite the lateness of her friend. What a surprise to see him and after all these years, too. She retreated once more into her medical school memories, but soon her thoughts returned to the reason for her being there. It was getting late. Where the hell was Suzalinna? Of course, she didn't even know what Agnes looked like, so that didn't help. She had been keeping an eye out for anyone hovering around, but there were so many potential Agneses that it was impossible to know. She couldn't just start walking up to middle-aged-elderly women and asking their names. She saw one woman going into the newsagents and thought she looked just the sort. She wore a lightly padded green jacket and a large handbag. Her hair was peppered with grey. The woman looked at her before disappearing into the shop. Cathy smiled hopefully and when she emerged with a magazine, Cathy stepped towards her.

'I don't suppose you're here to meet...?' she began, but the woman shook her head.

'No, I am not,' she said, and elbowed past.

Cathy shook her head and knew that she was blushing. Bloody Suzalinna. Making her look an idiot. Where was she? Perhaps Agnes herself had chosen to give the meeting a miss. She had no idea what Suzalinna had said to convince her to come in the first place. Cathy looked up at the clock above the exit. It was gone seven forty-five. She knew mobiles were discouraged in the hospital and feeling a fool for having stood for so long, she went outside to make a call.

It was quite dark now, and Cathy pulled the folds of her jacket around her and stood by the door so that she was sheltered from the wind. The number rang out. 'Damn it,' Cathy cursed, but maybe Suzalinna was driving. She stepped out of the way of someone walking towards her. 'Sorry,' she said, but the person hesitated.

'You're not Suzalinna?' the elderly woman asked. 'I saw you waiting inside earlier and was afraid to ask.'

Cathy exhaled. 'You must be Agnes,' she said. 'No. I'm not Suzalinna. But I knew she was coming to meet you. I think she's running a bit late. Shall we go inside a get a hot drink while we wait for her to join us?'

26

The blast of warm air hit them as the doors opened. It was a relief to be back inside. Cathy smiled at the woman walking beside her. Agnes must have been in her late fifties, or perhaps early sixties. She was short, and although she wore a thick coat, she was undoubtedly stout. Her face was rather washed out, and her hair, a light grey.

'Sorry about the mix-up,' Cathy said. 'Suzalinna's usually quite good at timekeeping. I don't know what's become of her. Here, let me get us both a drink. Tea, coffee?'

Agnes said that she'd have a hot chocolate.

'We'll sit over here. Then she'll see us as soon as she walks in. I'm Cathy, by the way. Sorry. I'm a close friend of Suzalinna and Saj. They've told me a good bit about the troubles lately in the pathology lab.'

'I don't know what she wanted to talk about,' Agnes said. 'She sounded quite insistent and knowing that she was Dr Bhat's wife, I wondered if it was something about him.'

'Oh, I don't think so. Suzalinna's been concerned about the team, being a consultant herself in the same hospital, I think. I realise that the department has been under a good deal of strain since Michael's death.'

Agnes grunted. 'And before that too. There was no love lost between that jumped-up little brat and the rest of us.'

Cathy raised her eyebrows. It seemed Agnes was more than willing to talk freely about matters, even with her, a stranger.

'Oh, it's probably terrible speaking ill of the dead, but few will mourn him. Off his face on goodness knows what half the time. You'd know when he hadn't taken any of whatever it was because his hands shook. Dreadful conceit and playing that silly Sara for a complete fool.'

'I had heard there were rumours...'

Agnes took a sip of her hot chocolate and winced. 'Absurd, the whole thing. A pantomime and both carrying on as if they weren't married.'

'What about the rest of the team? Did you mean to imply that other people had fallen out with Michael? I heard that he and the professor had had words. Was that because of his drug-taking or his lateness at work? Wasn't it the day of the meal?'

'Oh, you heard about that, too? Yes. He was often late, and rude to me more than once. Messed up some important results in one of the professor's experiments. He was writing up a paper and I think Michael mixed up some of the notes or something. That was just this week. Professor Huxley was furious with him, but that's only one example. His dictation tapes were scandalous at times. Thought he was dictating to Sara, and instead, I picked it up. In the end, I had to speak to the professor about it. The things he said in between reports!'

'What did he say in the reports?' Cathy asked, now sitting on the edge of her plastic chair. She had long since forgotten that her friend was meant to be joining them and the coming and going of staff and patients around them was of no interest. She concentrated fully on what Agnes was saying.

Agnes rounded her shoulders and pursed her lips. '"Darling" this and "darling" that. He'd make derogatory remarks too about the technicians, like: "I'm only doing this one, Sara dear, because Hughie's been missing from the department for the past hour," and then he'd go into the report. Nasty and unprofessional but Sara thought he was God's gift.'

'Do you think anything happened between them?'

Agnes shook her head. 'I can't be sure. Maybe. She denied it. It had fizzled out by the time we went for our meal, though. He started off flirting with her outrageously. I think he grew bored though as he became drunker.'

'He was drinking heavily?'

Agnes snorted. 'More than the rest put together. It was as if he was on a mission that night to spend as much of the department's money and get as drunk and abusive as he possibly could. I've met men like that before. The morning after, they blame alcohol for their bad behaviour, but it's in them from the start. The alcohol just loosens their tongue.'

'I understand the police say he committed suicide by swallowing something – a chemical, possibly from the lab.'

'Yes. I heard that too. They've asked a good deal about how he might have had access to it, and how he could have removed it from the lab. Someone's in trouble, that's for sure.'

'Surely, anyone working there might have had access to it,' Cathy said. 'I mean, it can't have been that hard to walk out with something.'

'A big bottle, though, and he'd have to pass my office. I see them all coming and going, you know? Anyway, the police already seem to know how the stuff got mislaid...'

'Oh?'

'Sara. No idea why she became involved, but it was her who was meant to send the bottle of whatever it was back. Well, it didn't arrive back at the suppliers and we can only assume that she messed it up. I don't know what she did with the stuff but it was her responsibility. Ettie came in one morning and asked her about it and she went as white as a sheet. Thought I hadn't noticed but I see everything. I know what happened only too well. She'd fudged returning it, that's what, and to save face in front of Michael, she probably had to hide the stuff. I can only assume Michael got his grubby paws on it then.'

'Perhaps,' Cathy said, not entirely convinced by this theory. 'I suppose I'm now wondering when he might have swallowed it. Do you think he might have taken it while he was at the restaurant? I know it seems unlikely that he would decide to kill himself on a work night out, but if he was drunk and maudlin, I suppose it's possible. People make bad decisions when they're intoxicated. If he'd been taking other drugs on and off too...'

Agnes's brows creased, and she rubbed her bottom lip with her forefinger. 'It's funny. I'd never thought of him doing it then. I assumed it was on the way home after the club. Maybe. He was growing very morose, as you say, although I can't see why. Everyone else was trying to get on.'

'Was there a time he might have done it in the restaurant?'

Agnes considered again. 'It's possible. Let me try to think it through. Sara and Jennifer, or maybe it was Ettie, went off to the toilet together. I felt sorry for the two young lab technicians that night. Goodness knows what they thought about it all. Spent a lot of the evening whispering away together or on their mobile phones. You know what girls are like these days?'

Cathy smiled. 'They get on well then, Ettie and Jennifer?'

Agnes again thought for a moment. 'Sometimes and sometimes not. Young girls can be bitchy, especially when there are men about.'

'But surely neither of them...'

'Had eyes on any of the doctors? Well, maybe not... I did have my suspicions at one time, but that's hearsay.'

Cathy waited, not wanting to force the indiscretion too eagerly.

But disappointingly, Agnes had moved on to other things. 'And that night was meant to be a morale boost, too. Seems ludicrous to even think of now. Anyway, you were asking about when he might have taken it. While the girls were away, and now I think of it, I'm sure all three of them were away together, Sara's coat got knocked on the floor. Another customer nearly tripped on it. A waiter was going to hang it up by the door. They were run off their feet though. It looked like the whole place was fully booked, probably because it was buffet night. Our starters certainly took forever to come. Anyway, Michael said to the waiter not to bother with Sara's jacket. He said he was going to get fresh air and he'd hang it up instead. He took it with him and disappeared for a good ten minutes. I think a few of us went to the buffet then. Prof Huxley seemed determined to get his money's worth. He returned with his plate piled high and said that he'd seen Michael outside, stumbling around on the pavement. "Be lucky if they allow him back in," he said to us.'

'Oh dear,' Cathy said. 'But they did allow him in again. I suppose that might have been when he took something, when he was outside, but it does seem unlikely.'

Agnes shrugged.

'When he came back to the table, how was he?'

'Well, something had changed...'

'Oh? How so?'

'It wasn't anything about him. Funnily enough, it was something about Sara. She'd come back from the bathroom and when we said her jacket was at the front door hung up, she disappeared to get it. She returned, and I wondered if she and Michael had arranged it just so they could have a chance to speak without us all listening in. If they had spoken, the conversation hadn't gone well though. Sara came back first, and her face was like thunder. I've never seen her looking so odd. Her eyes were sort of wild, like she was on the edge of hysteria, but when she spoke, she sounded completely calm. It sounds strange saying it now. I assumed they'd had a tiff.'

Cathy nodded. 'You may be right, by the sounds of things.'

Agnes repositioned herself in her seat, seemingly enjoying the chance to talk with someone so receptive to her ideas. 'Michael came back only a minute or two later after Ettie. She'd been off somewhere too – buffet, I think. He seemed to have sobered up a good deal. Maybe the fresh air had done him good. He was less gloomy and more like his usual smart-ass self. The others said they were going clubbing, and he immediately said he was going along too.'

'Who went clubbing in the end?'

'Hughie said that he was going to walk down the road and decide if he was going in when they got there, so I don't know if he actually did or not. The two girls, Ettie and Jennifer though. They were keen.'

Cathy nodded. 'And Michael tagged along? Did everyone else go home?'

'Well, as it happens, I know one who didn't. I shared a taxi with the professor. Gentlemanly as you like, he was. Wouldn't allow me to pay a penny of the fare. He dropped me off first. I live just on the outskirts of town. I got out and said my goodbyes and thanked him for the lovely evening, although I think we were all glad to call it a night and have the thing over and done with. Anyway, I was faffing around with my handbag.' Agnes reached down to her feet and retrieved it then, holding it up to show Cathy. 'It's too big really, but I won't get rid of a good bag just to adhere to fashion or whatnot, but things get lost inside the big pocket, see? I couldn't get hold of my keys that night and I was still standing in the driveway. The cab driver's window was open, and I heard the professor saying that he'd changed his mind. The driver wasn't to take him to the address he'd originally given but back into town instead.'

'Where do you think he went?'

Agnes looked at her hands. 'Perhaps I heard wrong. But I'm sure he said the hospital. Although why he would come back on a Friday night is beyond me. But listen, if you think the professor's involved in pushing Michael over the edge and causing his suicide, you're wrong. Others should hang their heads in shame, but I'll not have Professor Huxley's name sullied. Michael was a law unto himself. I can just imagine how delighted he'd be now if he knew what a mess he'd left behind.'

27

Cathy spent the night in turmoil. Admittedly, the suicide note seemed undisputable, but the more she thought about what both Suzalinna and Agnes had said, the stranger it seemed. Was Suzalinna right in what she had suggested? For Michael to end his life after a work night out seemed odd. And why choose that noxious chemical, when so many other less caustic, and presumably less painful, ones were accessible? If it wasn't suicide, there was only one alternative. Cathy caught herself running through the possible suspects, ticking off the opportunities and motives, as she fell into a fitful and unrewarding sleep.

The following morning she tried to call Suzalinna at least five times, but the phone went straight to the answering machine. It seemed so out of character for her friend to go quiet. Not turning up last night had been distinctly odd, especially when she had been so excited about the meeting.

Cathy found it difficult to concentrate that morning. More than anything, she wanted to tell Suzalinna about her conversation with Agnes. Admittedly, she had been annoyed when her friend had started up this nonsense, but now, it felt as if she had been disloyal in some way, by jumping in and taking over what Suzalinna clearly saw as her mission. Cathy would have called Saj, but she felt she had already put her foot in it with him so she decided to wait. Surely, if anything untoward had happened to her friend, he would have let her know by now. He would phone her soon enough with the post-mortem results of Sara Wiseman's mother, anyway. She'd ask him then.

When she arrived at work that morning, she hoped that the distraction of consultations would be enough to calm her. James had come in early once again, but she was still to find time to speak with him. He had left a message on her computer saying that he needed to have a word, but they repeatedly missed one another in the corridor in between patients. It was a complicated morning, and many patients had multiple diseases or problems.

By mid-morning, Cathy found she was running so far behind that she only opened the message from James warning her that her final patient for the morning was going to be difficult, as the patient herself, walked into the room. Cathy swallowed the sick feeling of trepidation, knowing that she was quite unprepared having not had a chance to read through the lady's notes first.

'Dr Moreland, I presume? I should've seen you in the first place.'

Cathy inwardly groaned. 'Please come in, Mrs Dawson. Take a seat.'

The woman was middle-aged and gaunt. Her cheekbones and chin were pointed and she seemed all angles and no smooth edges.

'I suppose he's told you,' she said, nodding to the wall on the other side of which James consulted.

Cathy shook her head. 'I'm sorry. I've not had a chance to look at your notes. Dr Longmuir's seen you already, has he?

When was that?' She scrolled through her computer, but the woman wasn't willing to wait.

'A disgrace, I told him. I'll be putting in a complaint. Frightening someone the way he did. Imagine if he did that to someone less stable than me. I'm old and I can cope, but what if he told some poor young child? What then? Imagine the parents and how they'd react.'

Cathy shook her head, unable to understand. 'Sorry? If I can just read what Dr Longmuir's said here...' She leaned in to scan the computer documents.

'Oh, just you do that! Goodness knows what excuse he's made for himself. A pack of lies, more than likely.'

Cathy raised her eyebrows and skimmed the typewritten records. James had seen the woman three times in the last month. On the first occasion, he had found an unusual mole on her back that she said had become itchy. James had booked her in for a diagnostic excision, which he had performed himself. He had asked her to return for the results the week later. That had been last week. When Mrs Dawson had attended, he had been forced to break the bad news that on histological examination, the mole looked to be suspicious. She would be referred urgently to dermatology, where she would need to be further investigated.

Cathy glanced up. 'How is your back healing now?'

The woman tutted. 'Is that all you can say? Have you finished reading it all? He wrote in there about the phone call the other night then, did he?'

Cathy looked back at the screen. James had written a single sentence. 'Lab phoned to say a reporting error.' And then in capital letters, he had recorded: 'BENIGN NAEVUS. NO SUSPICION OF MELANOMA. PATHOLOGY ERROR. PHONED PT. AND INFORMED. NOT HAPPY.'

'Oh dear,' Cathy breathed.

'Well, exactly,' the woman said, 'and how many other people has he said are going to die, only to call later and say it was a mistake?'

'I'm so very sorry,' Cathy said, and she genuinely meant it. 'This must have been confusing and very frightening for you. I'll need to get to the bottom of things. How are you in yourself? Are you all right?'

The woman seemed to soften slightly. 'I'm not all right, no. I've been to hell and back these past few days. My husband and I were up half the night discussing whether he should remarry after I died.'

'Oh, how awful. Listen, I really will pursue this for you. In the meantime, can I look at the scar and check if it's healing? Would you let me do that today for you?'

'I suppose so, although, at the moment, I'm unsure who I can trust.'

Cathy nodded. 'That's understandable, of course. These kinds of errors are incredibly rare. Leave this with me, and I'll try to find out what happened. Of course, you can still put in a complaint but let me try to look into it first, if I may?'

The woman disappeared behind the curtain, as indicated by Cathy, and took off her blouse. Cathy came around and looked at the woman's back. 'I'll pop on a pair of gloves and remove the dressing for you,' she said. The wound was clean and had come together well. James's stitches were precise and expertly done.

'I don't think you'll have a scar at all,' Cathy said. 'You can put your top on again, that's perfect. Leave it without the dressing on now and the skin can air.'

The woman joined her once more. Cathy dropped the paper towel she had used to dry her hands with in the bin.

'From a medical point of view, this is good. You've had the mole removed correctly, just as I would have recommended. The wound looks to be healing beautifully. Now, as to the reporting error, I need to look into how Dr Longmuir interpreted your results and gave you that bad news.'

'Cancer,' the woman said. 'Thought I was dying.'

'Let me reassure you again today, that the lab report says that the mole removed was entirely benign. There was no cause for concern and no reason to think it was malignant, or cancerous. I hope that at least puts your mind at rest?'

The woman nodded. 'So frightened, I've been.'

'I can understand that. And I can understand your desire to prevent this from happening to anyone else. Can I look into things this week and then, perhaps, call you? Can we say on Friday, when I've found out a little more?'

When she left, Cathy flopped back in her chair and exhaled. Oh, God. So that was the complaint James had mentioned. What a mess, and so unlike James to make a mistake too. She knew it had fallen to him to be the partner to steady the ship for so long now. Had she been so selfishly caught up in her worries with her own mental health, and more recently, the two odd deaths, that she had taken her eye off the ball? Had James been struggling without her knowledge. Had this resulted in the dreadful error?

'You saw her then?' he asked at coffee time. 'I'm sorry. I tried to forewarn you, but you must have missed my message. I wanted to have a chat beforehand. It was too busy today.'

'What happened? I've not gone through it all yet. Did you muddle up two people? It's not like you at all.'

He shook his head. 'No. it wasn't my mistake, honestly. Someone phoned me late on Wednesday from the hospital lab and said there had been a mistake. They said they'd be investigating it at their end. I don't know if it was a clinical or clerical error, but of course, Mrs Dawson wouldn't listen to that. I did try to explain on the telephone that she was shooting the messenger, but you know when someone is in a state, they can't hear you. She wanted someone to blame, and it was me. Then she refused to see me. That's why you're dealing with it now, I'm afraid.'

Cathy sighed. 'It's a relief, really. I was unwilling to believe you were at fault, and I was right. I'll try to get some answers for her, and you, now. I promised I'd phone her at the end of the week. I don't suppose you've called up the lab again to ask?'

'They were doing an internal investigation. You know, as well as I do, it'll be a significant event and then, more than likely, swept under the carpet. Typically, though, it's us having to pick up the pieces, and they've tarnished our reputation.'

'You sound so cynical. Not like you at all, James.'

'Cynical and fed up,' he said, and then smiled to reassure her. 'You're looking cheerier today, though. What's the change?'

Cathy smiled. 'I met an old friend last night in passing. I knew him at medical school. Nice to reconnect. He sent me a message just now.'

'He?'

She laughed. 'Oh, come on, don't.'

What with all the concern over Suzalinna and Agnes, she had quite forgotten her chance meeting with Chris, but when her phone had beeped to alert her to a text message, she had pounced on it, hoping for news. Instead of being Suzalinna though, it had been him, just saying how nice it was to see her. She found herself a little disappointed to hear that he was just going on to a week of nights, so any opportunity to catch up properly in the short term was impossible. 'Next Wed?' he had typed, and she had smiled at the phone screen.

'I'm glad for you,' James continued. 'Glad to see you more cheerful and glad you've dropped this nonsense over Sara

Wiseman's mother, anyway. It was dragging you down worrying about it all.'

Cathy nodded, but didn't look at him. 'Listen, I'd better get on and start visits. Nice to catch up and I'll let you know what the lab says when I hear.'

Cathy jogged downstairs, guilt eating away at her stomach. If James knew she was eagerly anticipating the post-mortem results of Mrs Wiseman's mother, what would he say? After her conversation with Agnes, she wondered what the cause of death might be. If it showed that someone poisoned the old woman, well, Suzalinna had been right all along. Someone had surely also murdered Michael and it put Sara Wiseman bang in the frame for both deaths.

28

'She died of natural causes,' Saj said before she could speak. Cathy deflated like a darted balloon. 'Are you sure?'

'One hundred per cent. Mrs Golding died of cerebrovascular thrombosis. Her blood vessels were narrowed significantly, and she was living on borrowed time.'

Cathy felt almost dizzy with both confusion and relief. 'Did you check the stomach?'

He sighed. 'I did, not that it was warranted. Nothing of interest to you. She'd had a small meal of toast and scrambled eggs, if you must know. No poison of any kind, if that's what you'd been expecting.'

'Oh God, what a weight off my mind. Well, I'm glad to know all the same,' she told him. 'I'm sorry to have asked. Her poor family will be relieved too.'

'Were they concerned particularly? I thought it was just you?'

'The son-in-law was worried. Look, I am sorry, Saj. You've enough to do without extra PMs. I do realise that the lab must be hectic.'

'It's been pretty hellish.'

'Listen, before you go, I just wanted to ask... We had a lab report error. A mistaken telephone call about a melanoma on one of our patients, that then turned out to be benign. Don't suppose you know anything about it? Seems a bit odd. I can't remember anything like that happening while I've been working here.'

He cursed under his breath. 'As if we haven't enough going on and now a significant event to deal with. I apologise unreservedly for that, Cathy. I'll look into it for you. I can only assume that it'll have been a clerical mistake. Agnes has been snowed under with Sara being off. She must be stressed. She didn't turn up this morning either, and there was no explanation. Very unlike her.'

'Agnes isn't at work?' Cathy suddenly felt sick. 'What do you mean?' She thought of her friend, who she was to still hear from also. 'What about Suzalinna?'

'What about her?'

'Where is she? She was meant to meet me last night but didn't show. I've left a dozen messages on her phone but she's not returned any of them.'

'Odd. She and I have been having some issues, as you know...'

'Oh God, but tell me you've seen her. She was at home last night, wasn't she?'

'As it happens, no. She didn't say it was you she was meeting when she left the house. I've not heard from her since. She said she might go and stay with one of her friends after work.'

'What friend? Who was she staying with? Saj, none of this adds up.'

'Cathy, please don't take offence, but really, this is between her and me. We both needed some breathing space for a few days. I'd be grateful if you'd allow us that.'

'Aren't you worried? I have a horrible feeling...'

'Cathy,' he interrupted. 'I've already pandered to your *horrible feelings*. I did this post-mortem as a favour because of just that. Now, please have the decency to respect my privacy.'

Cathy swallowed. 'I'm sorry...' But she was only answered by the dialling tone.

What on earth was going on? Agnes hadn't turned up for work and then Suzalinna, who was meant to be meeting her, had disappeared too. She didn't buy into this nonsense about her staying with a friend. Who would she stay with other than Cathy herself? No, something wasn't right.

The more she thought about it, the more worried she became. Had Suzalinna been digging around, asking too many awkward questions about Michael's death? Cathy had ignored her friend's plea that it had been murder, but why then had she vanished?

She thought of her phone conversation with Suzalinna the previous night. It was the last time they had spoken and was when her friend had asked if she would like to join her in meeting Agnes. Suzalinna had said to her that she had already spoken to Jennifer and Ettie about Michael's death. Cathy had mentioned the professor and Hughie, but her friend had said Agnes was the next in line. Or had she? Cathy thought again. What had Suzalinna actually said? She was going to meet her at seven-fifteen, but that was after something else. Cathy wished now that she had paid more attention to what her friend was saying. Had Suzalinna planned to meet someone before her and Agnes? And what of Agnes? Where had she gone? The whole thing was becoming more and more ludicrous.

Cathy sat with her head in her hands. What was she meant to do now?

29

Sara got up from the bed and touched the sleeve of John's suit jacket. It was hanging on the door of the wardrobe. He didn't wear suits normally. He'd feel itchy and awkward later in the crematorium.

The last few days had been torture. She hoped that her mother's funeral would bring some closure. The service would be a simple one. Small, without fuss. A post-mortem had seemed so undignified, so invasive. They explained why, of course. The doctor wanted to be sure. Anyone dying unexpectedly would need the precise cause of death confirmed. Sara had prepared for the worst, and when the doctor rang again to tell her it was fine, she felt deflated. After all, what was life now without Michael in it?

As she sat in her bedroom, her black dress still lying on the bed, she pictured her mother lying on one of the cold metal tables in the hospital. She wondered who had done the post-mortem. Surely not Dr Bhat or the professor. Her mother would have gone to a different hospital. That was only right. Sara thought of the room she had entered with such trepidation only months before and wondered if it was like the one her mother had been wheeled into. It would smell of disinfectant. She wondered how the doctors didn't gag with it. In their pathology lab, there was a line of tables, four, all spaced respectfully apart, maybe a metre or two between them to allow the doctors to move around. They were shaped so that the person being examined nestled in a hollow, like a protective cocoon. But the plughole at the base inversed any such romantic notion. To drain away the blood. Sara shook her head, trying to remove the image.

She couldn't allow herself to think of them cutting her mother. She would only see them washing down the shiny metallic surface at the end. They had a tap, more like a showerhead. It was hung above the line of tables and could be moved along a rail-track system and used in all areas of the room as required.

John came into the bedroom with a cup of tea and interrupted this particular horror. She was looking out of the window, watching the neighbours get into their car to go to work. She noticed a line of condensation along the window edge in clouded droplets. The showerhead dribbled a little and splashed on the shiny, steel slab, taunting her.

Then, an image of Michael, naked and greyish-blue, came into her mind and she quickly forced it out. No. Not him. Not ever.

'Better get yourself together,' John said before leaving the room.

She nodded. Michael. Poor, beautiful, cruel Michael.

John had dealt with everything. All the arrangements. She should be grateful, but in part, she blamed him for everything. He had stepped in and done his utmost to make things easy for her. He had told her once more since that dreadful night that he forgave her. But for what? The irony was, she didn't even know. She should know. She was the one in the wrong.

Ten minutes passed, then twenty. John came upstairs again to put on his suit jacket. Her cup of tea sat cold and untouched.

'Come on, love, we're going in twenty minutes.'

She looked at him, her face expressionless. He thought she had killed her mother despite the post-mortem. The realisation suddenly hit her and left her reeling. How could they go on like this, living in the same house but neither daring to voice it?

'Sara? You need to get dressed. We really need to get going.'

She nodded again, but he could wait. After all, she'd kept him waiting for their whole marriage; what did ten more minutes matter on the morning of her mother's funeral?

30

'The police have found a body!'

Cathy's stomach lurched. She had only left her room that afternoon to check that no more emergency calls had come in. She grabbed hold of the reception desk.

'A woman. Found dead up by the hospital, apparently,' Michelle went on, seemingly oblivious to her distress. 'Stabbed.' Michelle nodded and then reached for the phone, which had been ringing for the last minute or so. 'Afternoon. Glainkirk Medical Centre, Michelle speaking. How can I help you?'

Cathy tried to slow her breathing. She still held the edge of the counter.

'All right, Dr Moreland?' Michelle hissed, covering the mouthpiece with her hand. 'You've gone awful pale.'

Cathy nodded blindly and not caring how many eyes must be on her in the waiting room. She stumbled along the corridor to her room and slammed the door.

Please. Oh, please, God. Not her. Not Suzalinna.

He answered on the fifth ring.

'Saj?'

'Cathy, I thought we'd...'

'Tell me it's not her. The police? Have they?'

He didn't speak.

'Saj!' she almost screamed.

'For God's sake. What is all this? I've just spoken to you only an hour ago.'

She tried to compose herself. Marching up and down the room now, holding the phone to her ear with trembling hands. 'I just heard they've found a body, up by the hospital. Oh, God. Maybe I'm jumping the gun but...'

'Cathy, stop this now. They found an elderly woman. She apparently tripped and fell down the stairs of the multistorey car park. I heard one of the lab technicians talking about it earlier along with some gossip about an attempted bank robbery in town.'

'I thought she'd been stabbed. Have you heard from Suzalinna?'

'Seriously?'

'Please...'

'She sent me a message. She's fine.'

'What did she say? Did she say where she was?'

'No. I told you already, we've fallen out. She's got a couple of days off work and she's gone to think things through. She said she was safe and not to worry.'

'What does that mean?'

'Really? You sound hysterical.'

'I am hysterical! I don't know why you're not! Something is wrong, Saj. She can't just disappear. She never has before. Why now? How do we know for sure that this body isn't her? She was meant to be meeting me up at the hospital last night. Suppose she fell on the steps and that's why she didn't show. Suppose someone pushed her! She didn't believe that Michael killed himself. Perhaps she asked too many troublesome questions. Maybe his killer caught up with her and put a stop to things.

They made it look like an accident, just as they had done with Michael's suicide. It was Agnes we were meant to be meeting. I spoke to her. She had a lot of ugly things to say about Michael. What if before meeting me, she shoved Suzalinna down the stairs? She has Suz's phone and to allow herself more time to escape, she's sent you this false message. She's missing too now, isn't she? She knows the police will catch up with her soon.'

He sighed and when he spoke, his voice was quite cold. It reminded her of when she had last been at their house. He had spoken to Suzalinna in the same detached, unemotional kind of way. 'Right, I hate to do this. Is James with you? I assume you're at work. Please, can you speak to him? You're not well. I think you must be stressed.'

'Oh, Saj, please don't...'

'I'm sorry. I've told you all I know. Now, I've asked you already to stop interfering in this business. I won't insult your intelligence and repeat myself. Please seek help. James will look after you. Perhaps you shouldn't be at work just now. I'm sorry, Cathy. Really, I am. I can only deal with so much.'

The phone line went dead.

Well, Cathy reflected as she looked out of her window that late afternoon. That was that. She had truly burnt her bridges with him. To be hung up on once was bad enough, but twice in the space of a day, was pretty damning. Not knowing what else she should do, she impulsively rang the A&E department and asked to speak to Brodie, Suzalinna's senior registrar.

'What's up, Cathy?' he asked when the nurse who had taken the call found him. 'If you're after Dr Bhat, she's off for a few days.'

'No, I had heard she was away, Brodie. I don't suppose she's been in contact?'

'She's not, no. But I wasn't expecting her to be. Is something wrong?'

Cathy had been holding her breath and now let it out with a sigh. The body had not been Suzalinna then. Brodie would have heard. 'No, it's fine, really. Listen, I heard there was an accident in one of the car parks. I don't suppose...'

He groaned. 'Yes. She came into us. Nasty, but not a chance of saving her.'

'What happened?' she asked, knowing she had no right to do so. But Brodie seemed only too happy to talk.

'Sounds like she fell down the steps in car park nine. One of the car park attendants found her in the early hours. Shortest ambulance ride in history to get her across here, but she was unconscious and died in resus. Catastrophic head injury. Better she didn't live, she would have had appalling brain damage.'

'Not a stabbing?'

'No. Who told you that?'

'It doesn't matter. Listen, who was she? A visitor to the hospital or one of the staff, do you know?'

'It's taken the police a while but they've just informed her husband and he's been up to identify her.'

Cathy held her breath once more, but she was now quite certain what he was going to say.

'Funny,' Brodie continued. 'Not had much luck recently. I heard that one of their doctors killed himself last week too. It was a medical secretary who died. Goodness knows why she was here last night, anyway. Maybe visiting someone.'

Cathy waited, knowing it could only be one person.

'Agnes,' Brodie said. 'Her name was Agnes Simpson.'

Yes. Of course, it had to be her.

She thanked him for his time and replaced the phone, staring blankly ahead. So many coincidences. But none of them made sense. A suicide and an accidental death in the space of a week. It seemed just too unlucky for one department to suffer so greatly. No, Cathy thought to herself. It wasn't coincidental. She had been foolish not to listen to her friend. Of course, Suzalinna had behaved idiotically, digging around and asking imprudent questions, but something very odd was going on in the pathology lab. Two dead and now, having tried to uncover the truth, Suzalinna was missing as well.

It was horrifying to think that after speaking with her only last night, Agnes had, by the sounds of things, returned to her car, only to meet her assailant on the concrete stairwell. Cathy grimaced. Had she put up a fight, or been so unaware that she had no time to do so?

Cathy wondered what the police had thought of it. Had they really fallen for the murderer's ploy? Surely, she and Suzalinna couldn't be the only two people whose suspicions had been aroused. But then, how dreadful and unlikely was the alternative? A double murderer in their midst. It was almost too appalling to contemplate.

Cathy crossed her room and looked in the mirror. She knew she was pale, even discounting the strip lighting. Her fists clenched involuntarily. She had to find her friend and stop this going any further. Michael Croft and Agnes Simpson had been murdered in cold blood. She had already blown her only chance of getting inside information at the pathology lab, unfortunately. There was no way Saj would entertain it. She'd have to be more inventive if she was to get to the bottom of things...

31

Cathy waited for the call to be accepted. When it was, she spoke with more authority than she felt. 'Is that the pathology department? Can I speak to one of your lab technicians? I believe his name is Hugh...? Oh yes, Hughie. Thank you.' Her heart rate quickened as she waited for him to be found. She wondered who she had just spoken to, a fill-in secretary, she presumed, given that Agnes was now dead, and Sara was still off on leave. When he spoke, she was a little surprised by his voice. He sounded strained, but decidedly young.

'Can I help?' he asked. 'This is Hugh Graham.'

'Oh hello. This is Argon Chemical Supplies,' she said, biting her bottom lip and hating herself for the untruth. 'I wanted to ask if there had been any further development in locating the mislaid products?'

'Argon?' he asked with what she thought was a hint of suspicion.

'It's the universal name of the entire company,' Cathy said quickly. 'Yes. We had communications with the police and I wondered, you see...'

'Right. Yes, I was a little confused. I thought it was Klava we were dealing with. No, unfortunately, there's been no sign.'

'Looking back at our records, this isn't the first time...' Cathy willed her hunch to be correct. Saj had said as much over dinner. 'It wasn't the first time they had had problems with missing chemicals from our lab,' he had said. Hughie, having had an odd falling out with the professor the day of the meal out seemed the most likely candidate to be behind something of the sort.

Hughie stammered and she knew she had been right. 'I– I, well, actually, I think it's the courier at fault.'

'I see. It seems odd given that we've had no issues with our other customers. Perhaps if I spoke with the doctor in charge. Is it Professor...?'

Cathy thought he sounded as if he was about to have a fit. 'A misunderstanding,' he finally spat out, after spluttering and coughing. 'I'm lead technician and I'll be sure to look into it from my end. This won't happen again; I can assure you.'

'Good. I just wanted that clarified,' Cathy said, now warming to the role. 'These chemicals are expensive and dangerous. We can't allow for any "mistakes" of this kind to happen.'

'No. I see. I'm sorry. What did you say your name was again?'

Cathy swallowed and, not knowing what else to do, slammed the phone down. Her hands were shaking, but she smiled.

So, she had been right, and it seemed that Hughie had a guilty conscience. Cathy knew that rumour had it that Michael had been taking drugs. Suzalinna had spoken with Jennifer or Ettie about it, and they had said it was common knowledge. Was it possible then that Hughie had been supplying the young doctor with them, by siphoning off supplies sent to the lab? But Cathy shook her head. Nice though the theory seemed, it didn't add up. For one thing, Michael would be perfectly capable of getting his drugs without involving a lowly lab technician and thus, potentially opening himself up to blackmail at the other man's hands. But more importantly, Cathy knew that the chemicals that the lab was dealing with, weren't the type of things that any drug user would want. Most would be caustic and unpleasant, hardly the sort of thing to take for enjoyment.

'I need to do some reading tonight,' she told herself.

As she logged on to her home computer, she wished she hadn't blown her bridges with Saj. He had sent her a brief text message to apologise and to say that Suzalinna had texted again and was fine, but Cathy remained unconvinced. She appreciated that he was trying to soften it, but Saj's text had been to the point. He had not signed it at all with anything other than a full stop. That meant a full stop to her interfering, too.

Without an insider at the lab, it was very difficult to infiltrate without arousing suspicion. Cathy had already taken a big risk phoning Hughie and pretending to be one of their chemical suppliers. But she had had a feeling about Hughie from the start. Saj had said that he had been quite rude about Michael, even after he had died. 'More trouble than he was worth,' he had apparently said to Saj. Then, of course, there was Agnes's revelation. She had heard Michael's comments about Hughie on his dictation tape. He had been missing from the department, according to Michael, and that was why he was doing the dictation for him. Well, there were a whole host of different things Hughie might have been up to. Cathy had known it was something dishonest and now, it seemed, she had been right.

Cathy sat up late into the night, scanning the online chemical information sheets on the stains and substances the pathology labs might have in stock. She focused on one in particular. Sodium Azide, the compound responsible for

Michael's death. It apparently existed as an odourless white solid but when mixed with water, rapidly changed to a toxic gas. It was so reactive that even coming into contact with certain metals would convert it to a deadly, explosive vapour. No one had died with breathing difficulty though, Cathy thought, but reading on, she saw that in its powdered form, if accidentally ingested, it would prove fatal as well.

'I wonder why it was wrong then...' she thought aloud, remembering that it was the chemical intended for returning to the suppliers. But as she continued to read, she thought she saw. It seemed that it was not only used in laboratory medicine but also car airbags. Perhaps they had sent the industrial-strength then. But it still didn't explain what Hughie had been up to with the chemicals in the past. Cathy couldn't see any reason for him procuring Sodium Azide for his personal use, anyway.

With little else to go on, she closed her laptop. It was gone past midnight but she was still too restless to sleep. She wondered if Chris was up, and remembered that he was on a night shift.

'Cathy?' he asked when the switchboard put her through.

'Thought I'd give you a bleep to shake you up.' She laughed. 'Is it busy? I couldn't settle and I thought I'd chance it, seeing as I knew you'd probably be awake.'

'Not busy at all. You're my first call of the night. I checked in with the FY2 and she's coping fine. Ward's peaceful for once. You know I'm in one of the on-call suites up on level seven. It's nice. Far fancier than I'm used to in Australia. Come over if you really can't sleep. I'd be glad of the company. I'm dreadful on nights. I know I should catnap while it's quiet, but I can't.'

In her heart, she knew she should laugh off the suggestion.

'I'm boiling the kettle now,' he said. 'You told me you're only a few minutes down the road. We'll have a proper catch-up, instead of waiting until next week.'

Cathy glanced around her room. The shadows seemed inexplicably long. The thought of another sleepless night worrying about her missing friend and the horrible mystery she had become so embroiled in, was too much.

'I'll be with you in ten,' she said.

32

He was dressed in green baggy scrubs. Cathy smiled recalling the set she had secretly kept herself all these years, despite having finished her hospital medicine days. Comfy pyjamas, she had thought at the time, but she rarely wore them now, preferring to leave her junior doctor days as a distant memory.

'Well? What do you think?' He gestured to the room. 'It's one of the new suites, apparently.'

Cathy looked around. A small living space with a kitchenette. A bedroom with an en suite was visible through a door to the right. She laughed. 'A bit different from our old house officer days, isn't it? The poky little on-call rooms we used to end up in at the end of some basement corridor...'

He interrupted. 'That was if we were lucky! I slept on the empty ward beds a few times when the nurses took pity on me.'

'Were you in doctors' accommodation, I can't remember? I was for three months but they discovered asbestos in the roof and I had to move out.'

He grunted and shook his head. 'I can well believe it. No. I lived in town. Kettle's just boiled. Coffee?'

He indicated that she should sit, and she did so, on one of the low hospital sofa chairs.

'It feels funny,' she said, settling herself. 'Funny to be in the bowels of the hospital. Funny to see you too.'

'Funny, but good?' He glanced around at her; a spoon poised over one of the coffee cups. 'I'm sorry we lost touch.'

She sighed. 'Me too. I lost touch with most of our year.'

'But not Suzalinna?' He looked at her quizzically. 'Something's up. I knew as soon as you called.'

She nodded, unsure where to begin, or if she should at all.

He brought the mugs to the table and turned the handle of hers so that she could take it easily. They sat in silence for some minutes.

'Well, first off, you can start by telling me what's been happening since medical school,' he finally said. 'You've told me about your practice in town, but, well, I assume you're not married? Any kids?'

She smiled and shook her head. 'No, no one. And you?'

'I told you that already. What I had fell apart in Australia. It's a fresh start here.'

'And plastics is where it's at? Do you like the work? What did you specialise in?'

'Burns and yes. It's everything I wanted, as far as that's concerned. I was lucky to end up back here, really. The job came up, and it seemed like fate.'

'How long are you here for, do you know?'

She realised that the surgical rotations were unlikely to be permanent unless he secured a consultant position.

'Between six and twelve months and then, we'll see. I'm fortunate to have been given the training post.'

She nodded and sipped her coffee.

'So, tell me...' he began. 'Someone said you'd been...'

She looked up at him, hearing his tone change. His eyes were a pale grey and full of what looked like concern. He'd heard, of course.

'The bipolar? This place doesn't change at all then.'

He shifted in his seat. 'No, Cathy, not that, but you'll forgive me for being interested. I asked around after we bumped into one another. I was so pleased to see you, you know? I'm sorry, perhaps I shouldn't have...'

'I'm stable, as it happens, if that's what you want to hear? That wasn't why I called this evening at all.'

It hadn't gone to plan. She felt sick and full of disappointment.

He leaned forward in his chair, his hands clasped. 'I'm not interrogating you.'

She smiled slightly and shook her head. 'I get defensive.' She looked at him again and then swiftly away. 'What you heard was right. I've not been well. Four years. I'm lucky to be practising still. Tight supervision. My practice partner has been brilliant. But I am stable on meds and I've not had a manic episode in over a year. There, that's my medical history done with.' She placed her cup down on the table too forcefully, and the liquid slopped up and over the edge. Her heart was pounding in her ears. What did it matter, anyway?

'Are you always like this?'

'Only with people I like.'

He guffawed. 'Cathy! It's little wonder you're single still. Talk about a tough nut to crack. The bipolar is none of my business. I wasn't asking for a rundown of your mental health status, as it happens, I was concerned about you. You said you couldn't sleep when you phoned. I wondered if there was something up, that's all.' He reached out and touched her leg. 'Cath?'

She flinched.

'I'm a friend, okay?'

She sighed. 'Sorry. I wish we could start again.' She looked at him properly. All these years since they had last worked together. It had been so long, but it felt as if they had shared so much of their lives already. That was what medical school did to you. Sights and stories that no one else should see or hear, packed into five impossible years. Facts tested and examined. Techniques learned and perfected. Friendships gouged deep into wounds that would scar them for the rest of their lives. No one else could begin to understand the desire to pass and the appalling fear of doing so. The first years qualified, the night shifts waking in a cold sweat with the bleep going off. Trying to remain calm, perfecting a detached professionalism that only dropped with alcohol. With drunkenness came insights into cases that would haunt them forever.

'I'm worried,' she finally said.

He sipped his coffee and didn't speak.

'Suzalinna's disappeared.'

He raised his eyebrows.

'She's gone. I was meant to meet her the night I bumped into you, but she didn't show. She hasn't answered my calls and now her husband won't either. They argued, but I'm worried it's something more than that. Where could she be?'

Chris shook his head. 'Well, she can't be far. I saw her only an hour or so before you that evening. I told you I had an emergency that night. Serious burns and trauma case. I ran down to the labs myself to collect the blood. I saw her down there, I'm sure. She was going into pathology. She didn't notice me but like I told you, she's passed me a couple of times in the corridor... What is it, Cathy?'

She felt suddenly light-headed. 'I think I'd better go,' she said mechanically, and got up. 'The labs. That's where she must be.'

'You're not going anywhere until you explain what's going on.'

But she was fumbling with her jacket. 'It's been good to see you,' she began.

'Fine. I'm coming with you then,' he said and snatched up his on-call bleep.

33

By the time they walked the length of the corridor, he was impatient. 'Will you stop half a minute and explain what's going on?'

A porter passed them, pushing an empty bed. The lighting was dim and flickered. The other man nodded at them gloomily. 'Evening. Or rather, morning.'

Chris smiled at him sheepishly and returned to Cathy. 'Well?' he hissed when the porter was out of earshot. 'You can't honestly think that Suzalinna is hiding in one of the labs?'

Cathy barely heard him and continued to walk ahead, her footsteps echoing on the polished floor.

'Cathy, please,' he persisted, hanging back. 'We can't go crashing in there. This is madness. It's the middle of the night.'

They had turned along another corridor and came to a stairwell. She didn't hesitate but plunged down the steps and then followed the signs for 'Haematology, Biochemistry and Pathology'.

If Suzalinna was down there, unable to get out for some reason, she'd never forgive herself. Her friend had been too inquisitive. She had snooped without attempting to hide the fact. If there was a murderer in their midst, and Cathy now strongly believed there was, then Suzalinna had put herself in terrible danger. She couldn't believe that she would disappear without telling her first. The idea was absurd and even more so when she was in the middle of an investigation. No. Someone from pathology was behind her disappearance. What had Suzalinna been thinking, going to the laboratories ahead of meeting with her and Agnes? Why hadn't she waited? Cathy had a sickening feeling that she knew the answer, but coming to the door, she forced the thought to the back of her mind and prayed that she was wrong.

'Well? What are we going to do?' he asked, now standing breathlessly beside her.

'A bit of night-time investigative work,' she said and smiled as the door swung open with the lightest touch.

The corridor that they found themselves in was in darkness, save for the thin strip of ground-level lighting. Cathy was aware that there was a window running along the first part of one wall. She peered to her left and saw through it the outline of two desks with computers on them and notes piled high.

'Sara and Agnes's office, I presume,' she said, as much to herself as to her companion.

Chris tutted, clearly unimpressed.

She came to the office door and tried the handle. It turned but didn't open. Cathy cupped her hands around her eyes and pressed her face to the glass, looking for any movement inside. Nothing.

'She's not going to be in there,' Chris whispered irritably.

She nodded. 'We'll try the lab itself. Come on.'

Now that her eyes were better adjusted to the dark, she could focus. On tiptoes, so that her heels didn't sound on the floor, she walked. Ahead, at the end of the corridor, was a set of double doors. The one on the left was again locked and she grimaced.

Was her luck going to run out here? But Chris, to the right of her, tried the other and it swung open with an agonisingly loud creak. Cathy held up a hand, indicating that they should wait. They both stood poised and listening. Cathy barely dared to breathe. Although the room was dark, a line of windows ran the length and the orange glow of the street lights outside defined the otherwise abstract objects before them. The only sound was the low hum of what she assumed was a refrigerator or some other machine. Cathy allowed herself to exhale. It seemed that they were alone.

They stood side-by-side in the main hospital pathology lab. 'Odd that it isn't all locked up,' Chris mumbled.

'Hmm.'

'But if she was here, she could get out as easily as we got in,' he continued. 'The labs have been working all day, anyway. She'd hardly be able to go unnoticed. I'm surprised they shut at night. I suppose haematology stays open and if there's any urgent...'

But Cathy wasn't listening. Her eyes flitted from bench to bench in front of them, taking in the microscopes, the equipment that she didn't understand, the computers. On the wall by the door was a huge glass store.

'The fume cupboard,' she said to herself. 'That's where the stuff was. The Sodium Azide. Well, it was meant to be there.'

She crept around the room, her fingers skimming the worktops.

'She's not here, Cathy.'

She ignored him and continued her search, peering under the desks and then down at the notes on the table in front. A set of figures she couldn't interpret. Perhaps he was right, and this had been a mistake after all.

'I wonder where the professor's research project is taking

place,' she murmured. 'Not here, I don't suppose, and his notes would be unlikely...'

But just then, Cathy was sure she heard a door creaking. She froze and listened. She could hear Chris moving forward in the darkness, and she reached out a hand to silence him. Trembling, she stood, unsure if she had been mistaken. But the noise came again, this time closer. It was the sound of footsteps approaching. Without a word, she grabbed Chris's sleeve and pulled him down behind one of the benches. Together they crouched, pressing themselves against the wooden stools beneath the desk. Chris's arm was wrapped tightly around her shoulders, but even this didn't stop her shivering. Her pulse thumped so loudly in her ears that it almost blotted out any other noise. If the person turned on the light, they would discover them at once.

At the far side of the room, a door that Cathy had not noticed swung open. An icy blast of air hit them and she instinctively pressed herself closer to Chris, now feeling his heart beating through the fabric of his scrubs. His breath was warm on her neck, but rapid and shallow.

Cathy peered into the darkness, trying to make out the other door at the far side of the lab and the dark figure that now stood there. Definitely a man. What was he doing there in the middle of the night, creeping around?

The man coughed. He had, what looked like, a briefcase in one hand. She strained to get a better look but in doing so, leant against the leg of one of the chairs, causing it to shift. Cathy froze. The man spun around and she shrank back as the light from his mobile phone torch lit up the floor just by her knees. But the light continued, sweeping past them and across the rest of the room.

The man tutted, and the light swung back towards the path

to the door. He walked briskly, and as the door closed behind him, Cathy dared to breathe again.

But she soon turned in horror at the unmistakable sound of the snib sliding home.

'Trapped,' she mouthed, and then when the footsteps had retreated from earshot, she stood up, brushing herself down.

Chris rose too, and she was unsure how he would take it. She smiled sheepishly up at him in the darkness.

'Thank God your bleep didn't go off. Looks like we're in a bit of a fix.'

34

'Oh, no, come on, Cathy, you have to be kidding,' Chris said, only then realising where she was leading him.

'Well, we have to,' she answered, not keen on the idea either. 'Come on. I never had you down as squeamish. I'm sure you've seen far worse over the years. Now that mystery man has gone, this is our big chance to have a proper look around.'

She pushed the door and the blast of cool air hit her once more. 'I can't believe he didn't lock it.'

'Well, why would he, when the main door's bolted? Listen, are you sure about this? What if we get caught? It's fine for you, but I work here. I'm hoping to continue working here for some time.'

She turned to look at him. 'You came with me. We're in this together now. I've said already that we'll be quick. I can't leave without doing a proper search, can I? What if she's here? How would you feel then?'

'She's not here. The only people in the dissecting room are dead.'

Cathy's face fell. She tried to swallow, but there was a lump in her throat.

'Come on then,' he said. 'We'll have a scout around and then I'm looking at the windows to see how we get out.'

Cathy smiled, but she felt anything but happy. What if they found Suzalinna and... But it was too awful to contemplate. Instead, she took a deep breath.

'No windows in this room, anyway. We're okay to turn on the lights.'

She fumbled along the wall and found the line of switches. She flicked the two nearest and the room was suddenly illuminated. In front of them, were four dissecting tables, all thankfully empty. The polished metal reflected the bright overhead lights and Cathy blinked as her pupils adjusted. The room was distinctly colder than the laboratory and the walls were tiled and bare.

'I think I preferred it with the lights out,' Chris said.

Cathy had crossed the room. 'The store must be here,' she said. 'I suppose we have to.' She opened the door and, as she had predicted, there was a smaller room lined with doored-hatches where she knew the cadavers would be laid out before or after the post-mortem while waiting for the undertakers' collection.

Chris was behind her and she was now shaking uncontrollably.

'No, Cathy, really?'

She looked imploringly at him.

'Wait through there. I'll check.'

She didn't argue, but turned and stood with her back to the door, listening as he pulled each hatch and checked for her friend. It didn't take him long, but by the time he returned, his face pale and serious, she was crying.

'She's not there, silly,' he said, and squeezed her arm. 'Come on, stop that nonsense. I thought you wanted to have a look around for clues or whatever. Then we need to go.'

His bleep suddenly sounded, and they both jumped and

then laughed. She dabbed at her eyes, relieved and embarrassed.

The phone was mounted on the wall. He quickly crossed the room and glanced around at her before lifting the receiver. 'I need to take it. Are you okay?'

She nodded.

While he answered his call, she looked around more thoroughly. Suzalinna wasn't there, but was there anything that might point to her whereabouts or the identity of the killer?

At the far end was a desk and on it, a collection of books and folders. The computer sitting there was turned off, but Cathy lifted the first book. *Statistics for Pathologists. Advances in Anatomical Physiology and Interpretation of Data. Tough going,* she thought as she thumbed through the pages. Replacing it, she moved to a large ring binder instead. Inside, the papers were slightly dog-eared. Obviously well-thumbed. It seemed to be a collation of figures relating to the causes of death found on post-mortem from the lab. Cathy saw the dates went back chronologically from only the previous week. They were handwritten, something that she found rather odd, given that most notes were now digitised. Perhaps it indicated that the folder belonged to the professor. An old man stuck in his ways.

She glanced over at Chris. He had his back to her and was still talking on the phone. It sounded as if he was advising one of his junior team. Cathy knew she must finish up soon and allow him to get back to his shift. If an emergency came in requiring his expert attention, he'd be stretched to make it back to the ward in good enough time. She flipped the pages of the folder quickly, preparing to move on to the next when something caught her eye. The word: Klava. Something in her memory stirred, but she was too overwrought to pin it down. Instead, she ran a finger down the scribbled notes. Klava was underlined and a table of statistics jotted. Cathy flicked back a page. The same table of statistics but this time, with the heading 'Actual Data'. What did that mean? The headings were the same but the recorded numbers, different. She flicked back and forward, trying to understand. Chris was finishing up his call. 'I'll be along and check on her within the hour,' he said.

Cathy impulsively unclipped the folder and removed two sheets from the centre. If they weren't recent notes, it might go unnoticed. She hurriedly folded the paper and stuffed it in her trouser pocket. As she did so, something from the folder dropped to the floor. It caught the light and glistened, a tiny circle of shining silver. Cathy bent and retrieved it, holding it in her palm.

'Well, then?' Chris asked, coming towards her. She closed her palm and pocketed the glittering circle. 'Anything interesting? I really need to get going.'

'Sorry, yes I heard you on the phone.' She shut the folder quickly and replaced it exactly as she had found it. 'We can go now. I'm sorry I made you come. It looks like it was a wild goose chase, after all.'

He nodded. 'The windows in the other room open out onto the car parks. We'll get out that way and I'll jog back in the A&E entrance, through ENT and up to the ward. I shouldn't be too long if you want to head back to my on-call room and wait?'

'I'd better go home,' she said, wanting to be anywhere but with him or anyone else.

35

She fell into a dreamless sleep almost as soon as she crawled into bed. It was gone 3am and she slept through her seven o'clock alarm, only waking when a particularly loud jackdaw shrieked outside her bedroom window. It took her a minute or two to remember the previous night's events and then, looking at her clock, she leapt out of bed. She'd make it into work on time, but it'd be tight.

As she towelled herself dry, having quickly showered, she reflected on the night before. What on earth must Chris have thought? She grimaced and threw the towel down on the floor in defeatism. She'd been an idiot involving him at all. With sickening self-disgust, she recalled him helping her out of the laboratory window. She had slipped, and he was forced to half drag, half carry her onto the grass beneath. Cathy groaned. 'What a fool.'

As she drove to work, she appreciated that the only purpose for Suzalinna secretly going to the labs ahead of meeting her and Agnes, was because her friend must have suspected someone in particular. Cathy had come to this realisation the previous night, but had been too obstinate to entertain the idea.

But, of course, it seemed quite clear. Suzalinna had suspected Saj. Why else would she sneak about the place without confiding her reason for doing so? It was the only likely explanation. She had wanted to check something, to either confirm her suspicions or dismiss them as lunacy. Cathy wondered what her friend had found. After doing so, she had disappeared. Did this mean that she was less fortunate in avoiding discovery than Cathy and Chris that night, or had the news been so awful that she had had to flee? The whole thing felt decidedly uncomfortable. All the same, Cathy couldn't believe Saj's involvement. She had known him for nearly seven years now. He had always seemed the picture of quiet humility. He was surely above suspicion. But what had made Suzalinna think otherwise?

Cathy waited for her first patient of the day to arrive. As she sat, she chewed the end of her pen, trying to think. It had to have something to do with the professor's project. Was the old professor up to no good with his research? Had it been he who had crept around the dark laboratory last night? It certainly seemed the most satisfactory explanation. She wondered if Saj was aware of what was going on. Had the professor planned to manipulate the figures to make his research appear more plausible or more impressive in some way? Cathy could only assume that if this was so, Michael had either witnessed it, having assisted in some of the studies or had at least suspected what was going on. Had Michael threatened the other two pathology doctors with exposure? Was that why the young medic had been killed?

She glanced at her computer screen. There was no sign of her patient still. Getting up, she crossed to the door and reached into her jacket pocket. Cathy was going to wait until later when she had more time, but she retrieved the papers that she had hastily folded the night before and took them back to her desk to examine. Carefully she laid them out, pressing the paper so that the creases flattened. Something in the centre of the page glinted. She picked it up. It was the sequin she had found the previous night in the lab. Who else wore sequins all year round, anyway? Suzalinna. Cathy thought of her friend and with a sinking feeling, she knew she had failed her so far.

What had been so important about the professor's research? Suzalinna had seen something of interest. But more worryingly, Cathy had to face the fact that if the sequin had come off, there was a strong possibility that they had caught Suzalinna snooping. At that point, had there been a scuffle?

'Oh dear.' Cathy sighed. 'I hope not. But what was she looking for?'

She pored over the documents. On the sheets of paper were two ruled tables with columns headed: 'Date, CHI' (this, she knew, was the number given to each patient to identify them. The first six digits formed their date of birth), 'COD and CV'. Cathy looked down the list. She assumed that COD meant cause of death and CV meant cardiovascular findings, as most of the recorded entries in this column described emboli or thrombosis in various sites of the body. Some of the writing was scribbled and difficult to decipher, and some patients had been asterisked. Cathy didn't understand what that indicated. She wasn't sure, but in two of the columns, the handwriting differed.

Her phone rang, startling her.

'Hello?'

'Sorry to disturb you, Dr Moreland,' Michelle said. Her voice sounded flat. 'First one's cancelled. She phoned five minutes before her appointment, so no chance for us to fill the empty slot. Typical.'

'Thanks for letting me know.' Cathy was about to hang up, but she stopped. 'All okay, Michelle? You sound a bit...'

The young receptionist sighed. 'My aunt. I assume you heard

about the explosion in town the other night? She was the one injured. The only one. Lived next door to the place. I've just heard that she died in hospital this morning.'

'Oh, Michelle. I'm so sorry. If you need to go...'

'She wasn't my real aunt. Just a close friend of my mum's. I'm fine, Dr Moreland, really. It's put a bit of a dampener on the day, that's all. I'm better here at work, keeping busy.'

'If you need to get away early...'

'Thanks, maybe I'll do that. Go up to see my mum and check on her. She's upset, of course. Oh, that's your second patient now. Julie's just checked her in. I'll let you get on.'

Cathy replaced the receiver. Had Michelle's 'aunt' been the woman Chris had attended the other night? He had mentioned the victim of serious burns. Cathy hoped that his absence from his on-call post the night before had gone unnoticed on the ward. She thought again of Chris and shook her head sadly. What an idiot she had been.

But she had her own surgery of patients to see, and perhaps that wasn't such a bad thing. Getting up, she refolded the papers on her desk and slid them into her drawer. Her detective work would have to wait.

She just prayed that her friend was unharmed. Of all the people Cathy knew, Suzalinna was by far the pluckiest. This gave her at least some hope. *She'd have put up a bloody good fight*, she thought, and smiled.

———

It was a relief to have the afternoon off. She spoke to James briefly before she left.

'Keep an eye out for Michelle. A family friend died this morning, and she was pretty upset when I spoke to her. I told her she should leave early if she needed to.'

James leaned back in his chair. 'Fine. Fine.'

She came into his room further. 'I assume all's well with you? We haven't spoken since that silly complaint mix-up. The labs were looking into it. I meant to tell you that I phoned the woman and explained what they had said. It was the lab's mistake and not yours. She's not pursuing it. Decided to drop the whole thing.'

He exhaled.

'Sorry, James. I should have said before. Had you been worrying?'

'Not really. It's a relief though. So,' he said, looking more cheerful. 'What is it you're up to on your afternoon off?'

Cathy's cheeks reddened.

'The medical school friend, perhaps?' James teased.

'Oh, definitely not that,' she said, shaking her head. 'No. A far less pleasant task, but one that needs doing. I've been an idiot. In my heart, I knew all along what I had to do.'

'Get disagreeable jobs out of the way and then you're not left dreading them.'

Cathy nodded. 'Yes. Exactly. This is something I've put off for far too long.'

36

In the end, she tried him at home first. The thought of revisiting the pathology labs made her feel quite nauseous. She was sure Saj had been due days off. He'd mentioned it only the other week when she had had dinner with him and Suzalinna. That seemed like a distant memory now. She cast her mind back to the night and recalled his jovial banter, but then, the sudden change in his mood when Suzalinna teased him. He had been under a good deal of pressure, but what had caused it? Was it simply due to one of his team dying, or something more?

'Oh,' he said when he came to the door and his face fell. 'I knew she wouldn't ring the bell, but I had hoped...'

He stepped back and allowed Cathy into the hall. Either he was putting on a good show, or he really was concerned now about his missing wife.

'Still nothing?' she asked.

He turned without speaking and led her through to the kitchen. He began to fill the kettle mechanically. 'Tea?'

She watched him go through the motions, taking cups from the cupboard and dropping teabags into them.

'You're just milk, aren't you?'

'Saj, for goodness' sake!'

He looked up at her – his eyes bleary and tired. He coughed and rubbed his forehead. 'Coming down with something. Must be the stress. I assume she's not been in contact with you either? I had hoped that you might have heard something.'

Cathy shook her head. Was he being genuine? She didn't know what to believe now. This past week had made her unsure of everything. Even people she normally trusted and relied on had become potential suspects.

'I'm sorry I hung up on you...'

'Twice,' she interrupted.

He smiled sadly. 'Twice, indeed. I'm at breaking point, Cathy. Honestly, I don't know what to do.'

He handed her the mug, and his hands were shaking.

'Saj, I came here because we need to talk. I need to ask you things. It's not easy...'

He nodded and perched on one of the kitchen stools, cradling his mug of tea, but not drinking it.

Cathy felt a pang of sickening guilt for what she was going to say. She suspected him of being involved, but looking at him now, hunched and exhausted, a broken man without Suzalinna by his side, she hated herself. Cathy took a deep breath. She must find out the truth. 'You know that Suzalinna strongly suspected that Michael's death was not suicide. She thought that someone on the pathology night out had been involved. In some ways, I agreed with her. Perhaps not at the start, but definitely now that certain things have come to light.'

He sighed and placed his mug down on the worktop. 'The police have already ruled that out. There was a note, Cathy. No one can argue with that.' He shook his head.

'Are the rest of the lab getting on with things so easily?'

He looked confused. 'The technicians? The professor? They

have to. We all do. No one's happy about what happened. Surely, that goes without saying.'

'Is anyone more distraught than the others? I was thinking of Jennifer or Ettie...'

'What do you mean? I struggle to keep up with your direction of...'

'An affair,' she blurted out. 'It all seems rather odd, Saj. I did wonder. Agnes, before she died, told me that the two women technicians were sometimes a bit competitive. Even on the night out, it seems that there was a bit of an undercurrent of nastiness when Michael took a phone call.'

Saj looked exhausted, but she wouldn't let it drop. 'I assume the professor wasn't of any interest to the two girls, and you...'

He looked at her savagely, only then understanding her meaning. 'Are you suggesting I was having a fling with one of them? Is that what this is? Cathy, I thought you knew me better than that.'

She exhaled. 'No, no, I didn't think so. I didn't want it to be that at all,' she said. 'I'm sorry. No, I do wonder about Michael, though. I realise that there were rumours about him and Sara. It doesn't seem quite right to me though, having known her and her husband for some time. I can't see her having the energy for an affair, especially as her mother was so demanding of her time. And if Michael was as arrogant as everyone seems to describe, I can't imagine him falling for an older, frumpier woman like Sara. One of the young lab technicians though, well, that's a more likely possibility.'

Saj shook his head. 'He was married.'

'People are idiots, Saj. You know that as well as I do.'

He got up and paced the room, and then, seeming to have made up his mind, he turned to face her. 'How can I take this seriously? Any of it? Think of Michael's poor widow. What would she think if she heard any of this? It's complete madness.'

Cathy was undeterred. 'But how can you explain him suddenly deciding to kill himself on a night out? It makes no sense. A woman scorned is a dangerous individual indeed. If Jennifer or Ettie thought he was making a fool out of them in some way, perhaps that was the motive to kill. Everyone had an opportunity at that table. Oh, don't look like that. I know he left a note. I've not yet spoken with his wife to find out the details...'

But Saj wasn't listening. 'You even asked for a late post-mortem on my secretary's demented mother suspecting murder there, too. Surely you can see how insane this all is? Cathy, you've lurched from one thing to the next.'

She grimaced. 'I realise I've been a bit haphazard of late.'

'A bit? Really, Cathy? Quite apart from all the stuff at work and then my wife upping and leaving me, you have been a bloody concern. I've been worried that you needed to see psychiatry again. I don't need this on top of all of the rest.'

'Saj,' she said firmly. 'I am not unwell. You are just going to have to trust me on that. And Suzalinna has not upped and left you at all. Something has happened to her. She was due to meet me at the hospital the other night. We were meant to meet your other secretary, Agnes, but Suz didn't show. I spoke to Agnes alone and then how do you think I felt when I found out the following morning that she's dead too, conveniently fallen down the stairs in the hospital car park?'

Saj spluttered and coughed. 'You're not seriously suggesting that someone pushed Agnes now, are you? That was a terrible accident.'

'Accident? Are you for real? Yes, I am saying it was deliberate. I honestly can't believe it hasn't occurred to you either. Suzalinna didn't meet me that night, though. She had another line of enquiry that she was following up on first. By chance, she was seen going into the pathology labs beforehand...'

'She's not been in the labs at all.'

'You're wrong. I found this.' Cathy reached into her jacket pocket and slid the silver sequin across the kitchen worktop.

Saj studied it and then looked at her. 'This is meant to mean what exactly?'

Cathy was growing impatient. 'Stop this!' she almost shouted. 'You know it's from her top. She's always wearing sparkling things. She has glitter and sequins on just about everything she bloody owns.'

'So, she went to the lab. She was probably looking to speak to me.'

Cathy rolled her eyes. 'Wives don't pop into work to say hello. Why would they?'

'Some do, and why not?'

'In the dissecting room? I don't think so, Saj. That's where I found this. In the room where you conduct your post-mortems, on the table by the side. There are books and...'

'You had no right to be there!'

'I need to ask about the professor's research,' she said, ignoring him. 'It could be of vital importance. Are you aware of what the professor is studying?'

Saj's eyes widened, uncomprehending.

'Suzalinna was last seen going into the labs, Saj. I have evidence that she was looking through the professor's folder. Now, will you stop being pig-headed and tell me? You're as worried as I am. Don't you want me to find her?'

He got up shakily and walked up and down the room, plunging his hands deep into his trouser pockets.

'Cerebrovascular disease, post-mortem. Hypoperfusion and damage linked to clinical dementia.'

Confusion crossed Cathy's face. 'I thought that the contribution of vascular disease to cognitive impairment was hard to prove or measure. He'd need patients' clinical notes...'

He shook his head. 'No, he wouldn't. He was only doing part

of the research. He performed the post-mortems and documented the findings accordingly. After that, it was out of his hands. At the end of the project, he was going to step in again, collate the results and write a conclusion for the paper.'

Cathy thought for some moments. It sounded legitimate enough. 'Were you assisting him?'

'He asked me to give him the findings of any PMs I did if the results showed significant CVD. It's all perfectly legitimate. I honestly can't see the significance.'

'And Michael?'

'He was meant to be helping, but they fell out over documenting the results. I think Michael recorded something wrong. It wasn't unlike Michael. He was lazy. He didn't have a scientific mind at all.'

Cathy thought once more.

'Would Sara's mother fit into the study criteria?'

'As it happens, yes, but what's that got to do with all of this? What's any of it got to do with Suzalinna's disappearance?'

Cathy shook her head and then looked up. 'I honestly don't know, Saj. Suzalinna has seen something I haven't. I wish I knew what it was. Has the professor been acting as normal since Michael's death?'

'As normal as anyone else. I've told you that already. We're in shock still, especially after Agnes too.'

He looked at her imploringly. 'Where is she, Cathy?'

Cathy sighed. 'I wish I knew.'

37

Not knowing what to do for the best, Cathy went home. Saj promised to call with any news. If it got to the following day without either of them hearing from Suzalinna, he said he'd go to the police. Things were becoming complicated.

Cathy let herself into the house. It was cold, and she quickly went around, turning on the heating and pulling the curtains closed. She knew that there must be something odd about the professor's research. She wondered if Saj knew and was simply trying to hide the fact from her. Could whatever it was really be that awful? Cathy groaned. By the look of Saj, anyway, it seemed unlikely.

She reached across the kitchen table and looked at the two sheets of paper she had taken from the dissecting room the previous night. The two columns seemed to indicate that there was a difference between the actual data recorded and the numbers given to Klava. Cathy had heard about corruption in scientific studies. If the company had employed the professor to conduct the research, there might well be a conflict of interest. Had the professor been tempted to manipulate the results in return for a backhander? Cathy sighed. It all seemed so unlikely. The professor must surely have a reputation in his field of expertise. Surely a man who had gained such status wouldn't be foolish enough to risk it all for the sake of money. Well, thought Cathy, it would be near-enough impossible to ask the professor outright about it, but the name Klava had been mentioned before. She screwed up her eyes, trying to recall exactly where and who by. And then it came to her. Of course. It had been Hughie.

She had had a funny feeling about the senior lab technician from the start. Suzalinna hadn't liked him much either. She said she had met him on a work night out and when she mentioned Hughie, she had rolled her eyes. The missing Sodium Azide was still to be discovered, but having trapped him into admission, she already knew that Hughie had been pilfering the stock from time to time. For what purpose, she still didn't know. Cathy assumed that there was only so long that his deceit could go on without notice. Had Michael realised what Hughie was up to and threatened to expose him? Hughie had been messing around with something unsavoury, that was for sure. And now, it seemed, the company he had been taking products from was at the centre of things again, this time, with the professor's research.

'I need to talk to Hughie,' she said aloud, and nodded.

There was no way she could do it that evening, though. Cathy was exhausted, and she needed to think about how best to approach it. Deciding that the only sensible thing she could do was to get an early night, she made herself supper. As she carried her bowl of soup through to the living room, her phone buzzed. She rapidly put the soup down and ran back to the kitchen. Was it news of Suzalinna at last?

'Hey,' Chris said too cheerfully.

Her heart sank. 'Oh, it's you.'

'Don't sound so pleased to hear from me then. I wondered how you were, that was all. Any word on Suzalinna?'

'Sorry,' she said, and sighed. 'I thought it might be her now. No, sorry, Chris. Still nothing. I'm surprised you're even talking to me after what I put you through the other night. Rooting through the hospital morgue isn't exactly a fun first date.'

'Oh, it was a date, was it?' He laughed.

Cathy felt her face flush. 'You know what I mean. Anyway, I've just come from Saj's house. He's worried sick. Saj is Suzalinna's husband,' she explained. 'He's going to contact the police in the morning if we still haven't heard from her. Listen, I am sorry about last night. You didn't get into bother with being away from the ward too long, did you? I've been worrying about it.'

He laughed. 'It was fine while I was away. It was only after our little adventure that things kicked off a bit. Not a great shift, all in all, but sometimes it's like that.'

Cathy suddenly recalled Michelle's aunt. 'Oh, it's just occurred to me. I wonder, were you treating my receptionist's aunt? I don't think she was a relative, actually, just her mother's friend. She'd been involved in a fire in town. Michelle said she'd been rescued but died later in hospital. That would have been last night too.'

'Yes. One of ours, I'm afraid. Nasty. I didn't like the look of her when she came in. She was quite settled early last night but sometimes they go off. And when they do...'

'I can imagine. I'm sorry.'

'It's part of the job, isn't it? Anyway, I'm phoning to check up on you, but also to see if you're free next week. I'd have said tomorrow but I'm on until seven and I'm on lates the rest of the week.'

'Surely not a real date?' she teased.

He grunted. 'If it was, it would be a damn sight nicer than

your idea of one. No, let's not call it that. Just a meet-up, does that sound okay?'

It sounded fine, but as she said goodbye after promising to speak soon, she felt a sickening guilt. Organising her social calendar was hardly getting things sorted. Her best friend was still missing and two people were dead. Tomorrow, she must get to work and find out what was going on in the pathology labs.

38

The corridor outside the labs had quietened now most of the staff had gone home. Cathy had been hanging around for nearly forty-five minutes, hoping to speak to Hughie. She knew what time the labs shut and had walked to the hospital following work, keen to clear her head as much as possible before the planned encounter. Cathy ducked into a doorway to avoid being spotted by Saj as he had left for the day. As he passed, she saw how haggard he looked. Perhaps he was right to come into work and try to keep himself occupied. Perhaps not. He had sent her a message that morning saying that he was contacting the police, having still not heard from Suzalinna. Cathy was glad. It had been three days now and knowing that someone was taking her disappearance seriously besides herself, did lift some of the responsibility she felt.

It was interesting to watch the rest of the department leave at the end of the day. She had heard so much about each of them from Agnes and Suzalinna and felt better putting faces to names. A woman she assumed was the fill-in secretary left first, for she fitted no one's description: an elderly woman in low-block heels, with a thick jacket and scarf that she was tussling with as she came from through the swing doors. Not that dissimilar to poor Agnes, Cathy thought.

She waited another five minutes and then saw who must be Ettie and Jennifer leaving together. Both looked stylish enough to have attracted Michael's interest. The girls were talking as they walked by, and the taller of the two glanced across the corridor at her. Cathy pretended to be studying a poster pinned to a noticeboard.

She didn't get a chance to see the professor, which was a shame. Perhaps he had left early, or more likely, was working late. Cathy remembered what Agnes had said about his activity on the night of the meal. He had asked the taxi to take him back to the hospital. An odd request given that it was already very late. Had it been him who had almost discovered her and Chris in the labs snooping also? If so, he was clearly keen to work without the scrutiny of others.

She walked up and down a bit in the corridor, unsure what to do for the best. It would be typical for her if Hughie was working late that evening. But within a matter of ten minutes her patience was rewarded. The door swung open, and he emerged. She knew it had to be him. He was the right age and just as Suzalinna had described, with a ginger tinge to his hair and a square jaw. She was surprised also to see the skin surrounding his right eye was mottled yellowish-purple. What had Hughie been doing to sustain the black eye? Cathy took a deep breath and stepped forward.

Standing in the corridor overthinking how she was going to ask about the professor's research had only made her edgy, and the encounter was as awkward as she expected.

'Who did you say you were?' Hughie asked.

'Cathy. Dr Moreland. I'm a friend of Dr Bhat's. He asked me to look into Michael's death...' Cathy's hands shook as she told this untruth, but he didn't seem to notice.

'Did he? He didn't mention it. Why on earth would he involve you? I thought the police were sorting things out. It was suicide, wasn't it?'

'Yes,' she said hurriedly. 'It was, but I think, what with the difficulties with staff in the pathology department, he felt that rather than a criminal investigation being required, a gentler sifting of circumstances surrounding the unfortunate event was needed. That was really what the night out was for originally, wasn't it? To help placate some undercurrent of ill-feeling in the lab?'

'The labs have been strained for a while,' Hughie admitted, smiling slightly at her.

'Shall we walk?' she asked, thinking it might be easier to continue the conversation whilst not looking at him. 'I'm heading towards the car park myself. I'm buying a coffee on the way past; perhaps I can get you one?'

He nodded, and they walked down the long corridor along which Cathy had crept with Chris only the other night.

'It must have been a long day? The department's surely struggling what with being two secretaries down,' she said. 'I heard about the other poor woman... Was she called Agnes?' She glanced sideways, wondering if he would look guilty, but Hughie was looking straight ahead.

'Tragic really. Those steps up to the multistorey are slippy at times. Shame. And close to her retirement too,' he said. 'We've got a replacement secretary but she's more hassle than she's worth. Doesn't know where anything is or how anything's done. Sara's back in tomorrow though. That'll ease the pressure a bit.'

'She was off due to a personal bereavement, I hear?'

He nodded. 'Her mother. Yes. Not been the best of times for any of us, least of all, Sara.'

'Dr Bhat mentioned a bit of a mix-up with some chemicals that she was meant to have returned as well...'

He snorted. 'The stuff that Michael apparently took? Yes. Bloody awful. God knows what happened to it.'

Cathy looked sharply at him. The tone of his voice had changed. He sounded almost cocky.

'I suppose it's difficult to keep track of everything in the lab? Do things go missing from time to time, then?'

They had come to a set of double doors and Hughie paused with his hand on one. Had she touched a raw nerve? She knew she must have. What would he say?

A flicker of a smile touched his lips. 'Like Dr Bhat's wife, you mean? I hear she's gone AWOL too.' He sneered. 'I thought I recognised your voice.' He turned to face her, his eyes narrowed.

Cathy swallowed. 'I don't know what you mean.' It had always been a risk, she supposed. Having spoken to him once on the telephone, he might remember.

'Dr Moreland? Is that what you said your name was? Such a coincidence, you being friendly with Dr Bhat too. And are you still working for Klava, can I ask?'

'I– I think you've muddled me up with someone else,' she stammered.

'I don't think so.' He pushed the door but stood, blocking her way. 'I've dealt with far worse than you. What a joke, sending you here, trying to trick me. Just you report back to them they've got it wrong. The only person they need to keep an eye on is Dr Bhat. He's the one who'll cause trouble, not me. If they know that much about it, they should realise that already.'

He moved through the doorway. 'Lovely to chat to you, Dr Moreland, if that is indeed your name. Sorry to dash off, but I have a life outside this place.'

Cathy allowed the door to swing shut in her face. Through the glass, she watched his figure retreat. His step was decidedly jaunty.

39

Cathy felt sick to her stomach. How on earth was she going to progress now? She was still to speak to the other two lab technicians, not to mention the dreaded professor. It would be impossible to do so within the hospital certainly, having already aroused suspicion. God alone knew what Hughie might say to the others if he caught her hanging around again.

As she retraced her steps along the corridor, she reflected on what Hughie had said. He had quickly jumped to the conclusion that the company, Klava, was investigating the lab. Cathy already knew that he was to blame for the missing chemicals. A guilty conscience, she thought. But why was he stealing the chemicals, anyway? She supposed he would no longer be so stupid as to do so since it had come to light but still, she couldn't understand what he was up to.

She thought again of his manner, his sneering way of talking to her and the black eye. 'I've dealt with far worse than you,' he had said. What had he meant? Had he been beaten up recently due to his involvement in the chemical thefts? An alternative to this had already crossed her mind and was far less appealing. She could accept Hughie getting a dressing-down from some local mob, but then she thought of the sequin and her belief that Suzalinna wouldn't go down without a fight. Was Hughie responsible for her friend's disappearance? And if so, what on earth had he done with her?

The corridor was empty and as she walked along it the thought of returning home gave her a terrible sinking feeling. Walking even the short distance alone in the dark, made her uneasy. Being in the house with only her thoughts as company was not a welcoming prospect either.

She looked at her watch. It was six thirty. She remembered what Chris had said the night before. He would finish work in half an hour. She could hang around and wait... Perhaps, grab a hot drink. He'd surely not mind.

———

Chris laughed. 'Did you miss me that much?'

'I've just had one hell of an awkward encounter,' Cathy said.

She had bleeped his pager just before seven. He seemed amused and a little taken aback. 'I'm upstairs by the main entrance,' she told him. 'I didn't want you to go out the A&E door and for us to miss one another. You said you finished at seven, didn't you?'

Thirty minutes later, he tapped her on the shoulder as she stood looking through the long pane of glass at the front of the hospital, at the darkening sky and threatening storm clouds. She spun around and then grinned.

'You are jumpy, aren't you?' he said. 'Come on, let's get out of here and you can tell me what it's all about.' He steered her through the main doors and they walked into the night. 'I didn't expect to see you. What on earth have you been up to this time, anyway?'

'I know you said you'd be too tired to meet up sooner. It was an opportunistic call. If you'd said no, that would have been fine.'

He looked at her and she laughed.

'Okay, maybe not.' She sighed. 'I've been trying to investigate Suzalinna's disappearance. Saj has gone to the police now and I'm no further forward. Chris, I made a complete idiot of myself talking to the pathology technician, Hughie, just now in the corridor. I couldn't face going home afterwards. That's why I waited for you.'

'I can only imagine.'

They were caught up in the crowd as they climbed the steps to the car park. He had driven to work that morning and said he'd take her home. His hand tightened on her arm.

'Ahead of us,' he said softly. 'That's the widow there. The wife of the doctor who died.'

Cathy peered through the sea of heads.

'The one with the long, dark hair,' he said, nodding in a woman's direction.

Cathy looked. Even from the back, she could see Victoria was beautiful: tall and slim, her jacket belt cinched tightly around her. She was walking with another woman, perhaps another nurse from the ward. As she spoke, Victoria turned and Cathy saw her face: pale and tired, with shadows beneath her eyes. But despite her obvious exhaustion, her complexion was clear and her cheekbones distinct.

'I'm surprised she's back at work,' Cathy murmured, afraid of being overheard. 'How do you know her, anyway?'

'ENT is next door to Plastics, remember? That's where she works, apparently. Someone pointed her out to me earlier in the corridor.'

Cathy nodded. 'I wonder if I can grab her for a word. I've been trying to think of a way of interviewing her, but I couldn't think how to go about it. I don't even know where she lives, you see?'

'Haven't you had enough for one night? After how it went with Hughie, I thought you'd steer well clear of any trouble. Come home with me. I'll shower and we'll order a takeaway or something. A chance to talk about the good old days. I've got wine.'

She hesitated.

'Leave it for now, Cathy, really. You'll only make more trouble. Please. I wish I'd never pointed her out.'

She was torn. Cathy wanted to interrogate Michael's widow more than anything, but how could she begin to do so without offending the woman? The thought of Chris taking her home and them spending an evening reminiscing was a far easier option.

'I suppose...' she said, but frowned and bit her bottom lip.

By the time they got to his car, Victoria was out of sight. Cathy felt she had missed a useful opportunity and was quiet as the engine started.

'Oh, look! There she is again. She's in the Mini,' Cathy looked imploringly at him. He had already reversed the car and was now one car behind. 'I don't suppose you'd follow her?'

He sighed.

'Just to see where she lives,' she pleaded. 'I promise I'll leave her alone tonight. I'd just like to know. It can't be that far, what with them both working here. Please, Chris, for me?'

'You're impossible,' he retorted.

Cathy smiled into the darkness.

40

C hris glanced at her as he flicked the indicator. 'You know this is the last thing I wanted to do after finishing a shift?'

They were at a set of traffic lights and, by this time, the Mini was two cars in front.

'Shh,' Cathy said, trying to concentrate. As the lights changed, she nudged his elbow. 'Hurry. We don't want to lose her.'

He accelerated through the junction just as the lights turned red. 'For God's sake, this is insane. First the mortuary and then a car chase. You'll get us arrested at this rate.'

She wasn't paying attention but instead, peered out into the night, watching the lights of the car in front through the rainy windscreen. 'Left. She's signalling left. Better hang back a bit. I don't suppose she'll be much further. This is a dead end, isn't it?'

He pulled in at the side of the road and turned off the engine.

'You're good at this, you know?'

He didn't smile.

Together they watched the car in silence as it signalled, and then turned into a driveway.

'Told you it wouldn't be far,' she said. 'And a nice bit of town too.'

'Happy now then?' Chris asked, sarcastically. 'Can I turn around and get us home? I haven't eaten anything in five hours and I'm...'

She reached out a hand to quieten him. 'Look. A neighbour's coming out to speak to her.'

They continued to watch from afar as Victoria walked up the path to her house. Her steps were slow and laboured.

'She looks done in,' Cathy commented.

Her neighbour, an elderly gentleman, had opened his front door and was speaking over the fence. Cathy wished they were closer, so she could hear what he said. Victoria stood a moment in conversation and then, raising a hand to signal she was going in, climbed the steps to the house. Within seconds, she had disappeared inside.

'Probably just checking she was okay,' Chris said, nodding at the man, who now turned to go inside.

'I wonder if he was the one who phoned the ambulance for Michael. That was what Suzalinna told me had happened.'

'Why didn't she ring herself?'

'Panicked, I suppose. Goodness knows why she went to work today. Surely, no one would have expected her.' Cathy turned to look at him. 'You don't think she was involved, do you? Maybe she delayed ringing for the ambulance deliberately...'

He snorted. 'Don't drag me into this. It's your obsession. I couldn't care less, one way or the other, and the police are obviously satisfied. If she is a murderer, she didn't look up to killing anyone this evening, anyway, so you can sleep easy.'

She smiled. It was all rather ridiculous. Even she could see that. 'Okay then,' she agreed. 'You can get your tea now.'

Cathy ended up staying the night. It wasn't what she had planned, but the wine had eased some of her tension. All evening, they spoke. Cathy couldn't remember when she had last felt so comfortable. There wasn't the need to explain. He understood. They had experienced many of the same things at university and during work attachments when they graduated. So much of what they said brought back a mirrored experience. She spoke a good deal about Suzalinna. She had become so reliant on her friend. Now she was missing, Cathy felt lost. Rather than trying to dismiss her worries, Chris listened. He didn't have any answers, but it was a relief all the same. When it got to midnight, she said she should call a cab, but it didn't happen.

In the morning, they were both a little unsure of how to behave. Cathy felt guilty for allowing her mind a night off from worry and awkwardly got up and showered. When he came through to find her, she was wary. Why had she allowed herself to be so impulsive?

'I'd better get home and ready for work,' she explained, wrapping a towel around herself.

Chris nodded. 'Sure. I'll drive you, of course.' She argued, but he was quick to stop her. 'I'm not on call until later. It's fine.'

In the car, she was quiet. It was still early, and the moon was visible despite the sky lightening. He pulled into her drive and put the handbrake on. Cathy unbuckled her seat belt.

'Thanks for a lovely...'

Chris tutted. 'Cathy, for goodness' sake.'

She looked at him sharply.

'Well, come on. We're both adults. Neither of us is committed to anyone else. Why are you behaving like this?'

She opened the car door. 'I need to get ready,' she said, wishing she could be less difficult, but not knowing how.

'I'll text later, or better still, you phone me. If I'm at work, you can always bleep...'

She shut the car door. Perhaps the whole thing had been a mistake. She'd been too hasty to block out her troubles using him as a distraction. And now, she was left in the same position as before, still no closer to finding out the truth and still missing her friend. As she closed the front door to her house, her mobile buzzed in her pocket.

She threw the phone onto the hall table. But only then, she saw the number.

'Shit!' she screamed and snatched it up. 'Suz! Suzalinna, Is it you?'

41

'So?' Cathy asked.

'Oh, please don't be funny. I said I'm sorry.'

They were sitting together in Suzalinna's kitchen. She looked pale and perhaps thinner. In fact, Cathy had been quite shocked when her friend had opened the door to greet her. It had only been three days, but she seemed to have changed so much in that time. Saj had gone out to get a takeaway. Neither of them wanted to cook that night. Cathy saw him in passing when she arrived. He was just getting into his car.

'Pizza okay, Cathy?' he had called.

She had gone to him, reached out and touched his arm. Poor Saj. His eyes were tired but his face, awash with relief. Typical of him to slip back into his customary role of host, despite the mitigating circumstances.

Cathy grinned. 'For goodness' sake, no pineapple on it. You know how I hate the bloody stuff.'

He smiled.

Cathy wondered how she could have suspected him of being involved in Suzalinna's disappearance. She had seen how distraught he had been. Had she genuinely believed him to be capable of anything untoward?

Now, in the kitchen, she shifted in her seat. 'You have no idea the upset you caused, and London of all places.'

Suzalinna grimaced. 'I know, I know.'

'What were you doing down there, anyway? You've still to explain. I assume Saj told you that Agnes died the night you were meant to meet her? I spoke to her myself. I believe someone pushed her down the stairs at the hospital. But why ask to meet me at the hospital and not show? I know you were there. Chris saw you outside the labs that night.'

'Chris?'

Cathy felt her face flush.

'Now who's being cagey? Cathy, have you got a man?'

Cathy choked. When she was done coughing, Suzalinna looked triumphant. 'Chris Williams, if you must know.'

'From med school? I thought he was in Australia.'

'He's back. Plastics registrar. Anyway, that's beside the point. You're meant to be explaining, not me.'

Suzalinna's expression hardened. 'You're right. I was there in the hospital and I did plan to meet you and Agnes.'

'I found your sequin in the post-mortem room.'

Suzalinna raised her eyebrows. 'Did you really? You must have seen what I saw then? I'm surprised you didn't realise where I was.'

'Something to do with Klava?'

Suzalinna nodded. 'Did you read the entries in Professor Huxley's research findings, the post-mortem results? He's been sponsored by the company and he's twisted the findings to suit their requirements. You know as well as I do that there was something odd going on. Perhaps you didn't recognise the handwriting...'

'You mean it was Saj's?'

Suzalinna nodded. 'I knew he was in on it. He had to be.'

'I wondered that too. So, you went all the way down to Klava headquarters in London, presumably to ask some questions?'

'I'll admit, it was a bit stupid, but I panicked, you see? When I saw his handwriting, I assumed he'd been involved in the fraud. I knew Michael had been murdered and I did wonder...'

'You wondered if Michael had seen what was going on and so he had to be quietened? Yes. I agree it was a strong motive in amongst so many others.'

Suzalinna looked at her questioningly.

'Oh, but you knew that so many other people wanted Michael dead,' Cathy said. 'Have you forgotten all of your previous groundwork before you went off on a tangent? I assume Klava put your mind at rest, did they?'

'Well, no, as it happens,' Suzalinna said sulkily, her bottom lip protruding like a spoilt child's. 'They weren't too keen on speaking to me at all. I had to do a bit of digging to find out the right person to ask. They all refused my phone calls, so I had to wait outside for some time...'

Cathy snorted. 'Idiot. But I suppose I can't blame you. I ended up doing much the same myself with the lab technicians.'

Suzalinna sighed. 'I know it would be out of character for Saj to do anything fraudulent.'

'Have you asked him, outright?'

'Of course. He denies any involvement. He said he didn't suspect the professor of wrongdoing but he still can't explain why he contributed to the results. He said I shouldn't have doubted him in the first place.'

'I think the professor is still in the frame. Agnes said that the night of Michael's death, she overheard him asking the taxi to take him back to the hospital, rather than home. I wondered if it was to fudge his results without the risk of his colleagues seeing him, but what if he went back to fetch some Sodium Azide? He might easily have then met Michael as he left the club. The professor already knew he was roaring drunk. It wouldn't have been difficult to offer Michael a lift home in his taxi and during the ride, hand him a bottle of water, suggesting that it might sober him up before heading home to his poor wife.'

'Yes...' Suzalinna nodded. 'That would make sense.'

The front door banged, and they heard Saj coming through. 'Pizza delivery,' he called out.

'Maybe we've come at this from the wrong angle,' Cathy said, getting up to go through to the kitchen.

Suzalinna raised her eyebrows. 'How so?'

'I'm just wondering if we have concentrated so much on Michael's death that we've lost sight of things. Maybe we should try to find out who killed Agnes instead.'

Suzalinna tutted. 'Well, it was the same person, obviously.'

'Yes, I know that, but why was Agnes killed? If we knew that, it might at least put us in the right direction.'

'She knew too much, silly.'

Cathy sighed. 'I suppose so.' Absent-mindedly, she took a plate from Saj and sat down.

'I wish you were a more noticing type,' Suzalinna said to her husband.

He shrugged and bit into the pizza.

As they sat together, eating their meal, they quizzed Saj again, asking him to go through all he could remember, but he was at a loss. Saj really wasn't the most observant of people, Cathy thought. He had been trying to keep everyone happy that night to avoid a scene in the restaurant. He wasn't taking in details in anticipation of being questioned later. One thing that he confirmed was that Michael had been on a mission to goad each of them. It had been a horrible meal with a dreadful atmosphere by the sounds of things.

'And the professor's project?' Suzalinna persisted, now that she and Saj were talking more freely. 'Michael had been working on it. You must admit it looks bad. The professor was manipulating the results for this drug company, Klava. I know you said you don't have a clue about it, but I'm your wife, Saj. I recognise what your handwriting looks like. Surely, you must have known what was going on if you've written in the folder.'

Saj frowned. 'I've been through all of this with you before. I told you that the professor wanted the department to collate all their post-mortem results on cardiovascular patients. All I did was record the details of my ones. If you look, it's about half and half. I've been trying to take on more of the PMs recently but the data's been gathered over some months now. I didn't know where the professor was going with it. He'd been trying to come up with something meaningful for a while. Drug companies do sponsor research, you know as well as I do. It doesn't mean that it was corrupt though.'

'Why were you taking on more of the PMs?' Cathy asked quietly.

Saj shot her a look. 'He's nearing retirement, Cathy. It's what anyone would do.'

She nodded but didn't speak, and the conversation moved on. Saj said that he had heard that Agnes's funeral was going to be for family only.

'It's a relief really not to have to go to another. Michael's is in the morning. Awful. The department will send flowers to Agnes's family, of course,' he said and sighed.

'Anyway, let's forget all about it for now,' Suzalinna said, for once perhaps realising her husband's exhaustion. She smiled wickedly. 'Saj, did you know that while I was away, Cathy's been carrying on with one of our old medical school pals? She was just about to tell me about it.'

42

They were all there. Sara felt sick as she walked into the crematorium. It was a different chapel from her mother's funeral. The funeral director looked at her oddly when she got out of the car. A half-recognition. What bad luck, he must have thought if he did make the connection. Two funerals in such a short space of time. Bad luck indeed. She doubted she'd be back for Agnes's 'do', whenever that was. There was only so much one person could take and she felt very much at her limit now. Oddly, she didn't feel too badly about Agnes's accident. She had been a rather dreadful woman and they had barely known one another.

'Over here,' Ettie called, just as she had done in the restaurant that awful night.

Sara's hand tightened on John's arm.

'Are those your work friends?' he asked. 'Shall we?'

No! she wanted to scream. *No, not with them.* But he was guiding her towards the bench. Already Professor Huxley was getting up to allow them room. She hadn't seen any of them since that night. Sara swallowed back the nauseous lump in her throat. *Don't ask me how I am, don't...*

'Sara, how are you? Your own mother's funeral was just this last week too, I believe?'

She nodded and died inside.

John stepped in to save her. 'It's been a difficult time.'

The professor's face creased in sympathy.

I don't want your sympathy, Sara shouted inwardly. *Don't look at me like that ever. I know about you, just as Michael did. I know about your supposed research, the fictitious data. Even Dr Bhat was dragged into that. I know it all because Michael trusted me. He confided everything.*

Hughie was at the end of the row. He coughed and then raised a hand to acknowledge her as she turned. Sara looked at him and forced her mouth into a smile. He was the one she felt most pity for. Stealing, and from his workplace, too. Oh, she knew she had done the same, but for a more personal cause. Hughie, however, was up to something far worse. She hadn't worked out why he was taking the chemicals. The company had been on the phone to her three times since she had worked there, asking if the labs had located missing supplies. They had initially blamed their courier, but by the third call, she could tell that they were getting suspicious. Michael had known. That had been why he had teased Hughie in the canteen over lunch. She had only made sense of it after he died. What, or who, Hughie had become involved with, she didn't know. He had been edgy though, and she felt sure that it involved him in something very unsavoury, if his black eye was anything to go by. *Good*, she thought cruelly. He had probably deserved a dressing-down. Too smug and too conceited.

She looked along the bench as she stood, removing her coat. Ettie and Jennifer were together, of course. Ettie looked dreadful. Silly little brat. He had had no real interest in her. Oh, yes, she knew about that also. Her tawdry little dalliance with Michael. Ettie thought she hadn't realised, but Sara wasn't stupid. She was a woman, and she knew these things. She felt them more than saw them. Every time Ettie had been in the room with him, the energy had changed. They'd been casual with one another at work. It was almost too exaggerated, Sara thought angrily. And yet, he had been quite the opposite with her. Flirtatious, to say the least. Involuntarily, she shook her head, trying to remove the image of Michael outside the restaurant, walking up and down, staggering with drink. She recalled the words he had said. So cruel, so cutting. He had called her a desperate, old... Oh, God! She wouldn't allow herself...

She sat down abruptly. The professor had to discreetly move the edge of his jacket because, in her haste, she had seated herself on it. Sara flinched with the movement beneath her. It felt like the ground was unsteady, even when she was sitting down.

'All right?' John whispered.

Sara didn't answer, but stared straight ahead, still caught up in her memory of that night. She heard Ettie say something along the row, and Jennifer titter. Her stomach lurched in agony. Of course, she had felt slighted that night, but Ettie should feel more so. Sara had realised that the only person Michael could have been confiding in so cruelly that evening was his wife, Victoria. If the pair of them had laughed at Sara's expense, she could only assume they had done the same with Ettie. Childish though it was, this sustained her to some degree. It somehow made up for the hurt she had suffered herself. Yes, Michael was beautiful, but cruel. His marriage must have been unusual. The pair of them had possibly delighted in his ability to attract other women. He had strung them along for his own, and perhaps his wife's, amusement. How powerful and proud Victoria must have felt to keep hold of such a man, a man who left the opposite sex in tatters. It had been a dangerous game, though...

She looked down the row once more. All now sat solemnly. Odd that Michael had known so much. And in truth, each one of them had reason to be glad of his death. Only one person was responsible, though. Agnes had known, of course. Bloody Agnes with her game playing. Sara was glad she was dead. It had become messy but things were safe now. With Michael and Agnes gone, it might all go back to normal once more. She'd go back to work. Perhaps she'd not stay for long. Put in for a transfer to another department, explaining that she couldn't stand the memories. No one would argue with that. Maybe she'd stop work altogether. John's wage was enough. They could sell off the granny flat at the bottom of the garden, or even rent it out for an extra income.

There was a sound from the back of the hall. They all turned to see Michael's widow, Victoria. She wore a long, felt coat with a high collar. Her high ponytail accentuated her cheekbones and gaunt features. Sara looked down at her hands and concentrated on her breathing. She had despised Michael's wife and wished ill of her for months, but seeing her now at her husband's funeral was too much. The torture of guilt was all-consuming.

43

Life seemed to have moved on even though two people were dead in highly suspicious circumstances. Cathy had invited Suzalinna over that evening after work to discuss the situation. Suzalinna was just as frustrated.

'Why haven't we cracked it?' she asked Cathy for the hundredth time. 'We're both highly intelligent individuals. It should be so simple.'

Cathy grinned and rolled her eyes.

'Oh, Saj went to Michael's funeral this morning, by the way,' Suzalinna continued, taking a slug of wine. 'Awful. The whole department was there.'

'Including Sara Wiseman?'

Suzalinna nodded. 'Looked terrible, according to Saj. She's off work again, and Saj says they're getting desperate. The fill-in secretary is hopeless.'

'Agnes didn't sound like she was doing such a great job recently. I think she was preoccupied with something. I've not told you this yet, but there was a major lab error. Poor James bore the brunt of it. The pathology lab gave us an incorrect result on a skin sample. James had resected a naevus and was initially told by the lab that it was a melanoma. It was only after he had broken the bad news to the poor patient that the lab phoned to say there had been an error.'

Suzalinna whistled. 'If she was still alive, she'd have a lot of explaining to do. Saj would be furious about that. Do you think something in particular preoccupied her? Maybe something to do with the murder?'

'Yes. I wonder if she tried to blackmail the murderer, and that's why someone killed her.' Cathy sighed. 'Agnes knew too much. She was very vocal about it when I met her. She was outspoken and nasty about Michael, mainly, but why did someone want her dead that night?'

'She knew who the killer was. It's the only explanation, or she suspected someone. Perhaps the murderer saw the pair of you speaking in the hospital foyer. Maybe they overheard and panicked. If she was bragging about knowing so much, then, of course, she'd have to be silenced. She must have seen who put the poison in Michael's drink or food that night.'

'We have no reason to believe that. She certainly didn't suggest such a thing to me when we spoke.'

Suzalinna chewed her lip. 'I suppose the police must have checked with the restaurant and ruled that out anyway, but how else then? Surely they'd have done forensic tests on the glasses and plates.'

'Not if they thought it was suicide. There was a note after all.'

'True. Why waste police resources when it's a clear-cut case?'

Cathy nodded. 'Exactly. So, we need to consider what Agnes did see or know. It must be something pretty damning.'

Suzalinna sighed. 'I've no idea, darling. And how can we find out, now she's dead?'

Cathy considered. 'I've been to the labs, as have you. Anyone going in or out of the pathology department has to pass the secretaries' office. Remember she dobbed Michael in to the professor and Saj for turning up late? She was in a good position to see anyone acting suspiciously.'

'But who would raise her suspicion when they all work there? She'd hardly get excited about one of her team waltzing in or out. She saw them every day.'

'That's true. Would she have seen someone carrying the chemical away?' Cathy wondered aloud. 'Maybe not. Especially if they had a bag or a pocket. I've been wondering about that. Why take a great big bottle of nasty stuff away, anyway? It would be cumbersome and conspicuous. Far better surely, to siphon off a little into a hospital universal container, the type used for collecting samples.'

'Yes,' Suzalinna agreed. 'Otherwise, they'd be stuck with a whole lot of noxious powder, not to mention a highly incriminating tub with hazard stickers all over it.'

Cathy chuckled. 'I was just imagining someone burying it at the bottom of their garden. No, not a clever thing to do. I read up about it and it's unpleasant stuff. They use it in the car manufacturing industry in airbags. You'd not want it lying around your kitchen for long.'

She recalled Sara's husband's suspicions. He had thought his wife had a bottle of something heavy in her coat pocket, having seen her mother that night. Well, her mother had died of natural causes, but it was still possible that she had taken the Sodium Azide for a different purpose. Had she planned to kill Michael in the restaurant all along? Cathy had essentially written her off the list of suspects since her mother's post-mortem had come back clear, but her motive for wanting the young doctor dead still stood. A woman enraged, having been toyed with and encouraged in front of her colleagues, might easily kill. Had Michael flirted with Sara, giving her hope, only to drop her? It would have to be premeditated then for her to have the stuff in her pocket before going to the restaurant, and from what Cathy had heard, it hadn't been that way. Something had upset Sara that night, but how could she have anticipated it?

'No, that makes no sense either,' she said aloud, having contemplated the problem in silence.

'I didn't much like Agnes,' Suzalinna confessed, unaware that Cathy's thoughts had moved on. 'She wasn't very nice, was she? Trying to get Michael into trouble like that.'

'She was a little odd but he must have been a difficult person to work with.' Cathy sighed again. 'But we're not getting much further with it, are we?'

Suzalinna shrugged. 'I hate to say it, but it's beaten me.'

They sipped their wine in silence for some minutes.

'How are things with you and Saj now, anyway?' Cathy asked.

'Better,' Suzalinna admitted. 'I had to grovel a bit...'

Cathy grinned. 'Good.'

'Yes, fair enough, Cath, but you know why I jumped to that conclusion and something still worries me about the professor.'

'I'll agree, he is a bit of a mystery and I've still to meet him.'

Suzalinna snorted. 'You're not missing much. Boring old fart and forgot my name half a dozen times when I was sitting next to him at the last awful pathology consultant thing. He's your archetypal nutty scientist. Saj was the perfect husband and got me away from him and his nonsensical chatter. He saved my life by the second course and suggested we swap seats so that everyone talked to one another. Saj's good like that.' Suzalinna had a far-off look about her and a smile played on her lips.

Cathy grinned. 'I'm glad things are back to normal. You had me worried for a while there. I thought you were going to end up in a divorce court the way you were carrying on.'

Suzalinna shook her head. 'Don't be daft. No, I told you, we're fine, but I am still worried Saj knows more than he's saying. He wrote in the professor's notes. Even he can't deny that. There must be something we've missed though...'

'I saw Victoria, the widow, the other afternoon, just in the distance. I was with Chris. The woman looked awful. I had a niggle when we were parked outside her house.' Cathy rubbed her forehead.

'What do you mean "a niggle"?'

She shook her head. 'No, I can't place it. It was just a feeling that I knew something, or had heard something, that made no sense. It'll come to me, no doubt.' Cathy drank her wine reflectively.

'Cathy?'

She shook her head. 'No, sorry. I was just thinking.'

Suzalinna looked expectantly at her.

'Drink up,' Cathy said. 'And then I'm calling you a taxi home. I need an early night. Tomorrow will be a busy day.'

44

As they walked up the path, Chris squeezed her elbow. 'Funny way for us both to spend the day off, isn't it? I'd have taken you for a drive somewhere, but you do have a strange idea of a good time. Are you sure we should be doing this?'

She smiled grimly. She had seen that Victoria's Mini wasn't in the driveway. She was presumably at work, but she couldn't have asked her, anyway. 'Absolutely not,' she said to him, 'but I want to know about that suicide note and I can't bring myself to ask his widow, can I? Maybe the neighbour spotted something unusual.'

She had begged Chris to come with her in the end. Suzalinna was working anyway, but more than that, she had wanted him there. He had been with her originally when the idea had sparked in her mind, and for some reason, she felt that a man standing beside her might make the whole conversation a lot easier.

They stood side-by-side on the doorstep. It was cold and their breath came like a cloud of icy mist.

'Here goes, then,' Cathy said, and rang the bell.

'Yes, I'll talk to you,' the man said, shaking his head sadly. 'I'm surprised the police haven't been round to me. After all, I was the one who called them and I was there in the thick of it. You'd have thought they'd have wanted to, wouldn't you? Come inside. You're both doctors, are you? Well, it's an honour. I don't get visitors often. My family doctor's too busy to pop in these days. It's a pity, really. Come on in where it's warmer.'

He led the way through the hallway and into his living room. Cathy felt rather awkward having blagged her way into his house, but the man seemed delighted to have guests and busied himself making sure they were comfortable.

Cathy smiled and now that she and Chris were settled on the sofa, the elderly man seated himself as well.

'I should offer you a biscuit, shouldn't I? Would you like one? I don't get visitors often.'

He made to get up, and Cathy raised a hand. 'Honestly, no, we're fine. Chris has just finished a night shift and we're heading home.' She felt him move on the seat beside her and hoped he wouldn't say anything to contradict her.

The old man nodded and smiled. 'You worked with him; did you say? Must have been a terrible shock for everyone up at the hospital. I always say how nice it is to have doctors and medical folks living on the street. Makes you feel safer, but who knows what you people have to deal with daily? I suppose it was too much for the young man. Stressful career and so on.'

'I hear you were a great help that night?' Cathy said. 'You called the ambulance?'

'Well, it was the least I could do for her. She was in such a state and little wonder. I know she's a nurse herself, but the look on his face and the way he was hunched on the floor... She was going to make him coffee, but as soon as I saw him, I knew it was wrong. "Ambulance," I said. So I nipped back and called.'

'Did you know the couple well?'

'They kept themselves to themselves. They were busy professional people, and that suited me fine. When the house was up for sale, I'd hoped for reliable sort of folk. No loud parties and the like. I'm not saying there wasn't any noise, but on the whole, they were good neighbours.'

'So, it was really just in passing that you knew them?'

'Didn't have any dealings with him. She seemed a nice, quiet sort. Very pretty. I went round about the Neighbourhood Watch once and I did the bins for them. Last thing they needed to be doing was dragging their bin up and down that steep driveway after a long day at the hospital. The least I could do. She popped over and thanked me once. Said I didn't need to bother, but I enjoy helping people. Shame the street isn't more neighbourly, but folk have their own lives, I suppose.'

Cathy nodded. 'They were lucky to have you next door.'

He smiled. 'Well, as I say, I like to do my bit. My wife was a nurse.' He nodded to a photograph on the mantelpiece. 'Passed nearly fifteen years ago. She'd have enjoyed being next door to medical people. I popped over the following morning to see how she was. I'd been up early baking my cherry scones. Thought it might be a nice offering.'

Cathy smiled and wondered just how welcome a batch of scones would have been. 'I heard about the wallet,' she said. 'I believe you found that the next day too.'

'That's right. Didn't turn up until the morning,' he said, nodding. 'I went round with my scones as soon as it was getting lighter. Thought I'd tap on the door and check on her, see? She probably hadn't slept, anyway. Up all night crying. I've been through it myself, so I know. Grief is a dreadful thing. As I went up the path, I saw it lying there on the side of the path. "Oh yes," I said to myself, "what have we here?" His wallet, of course. I didn't pull it about too much. His hospital name badge was in the window section of it so I just closed it and gave it to her. She phoned the police straight away to tell them. Read the note while I was on the doorstep, poor woman.'

'Did he explain why he killed himself?'

'Said he couldn't go on. He had been unhappy and hadn't wanted to burden her with it. Terribly sad. She was in pieces, as you can imagine.'

Cathy nodded. 'And you found it by the path?'

'Must have dropped out of his pocket when he came staggering up the drive. No one had seen it the night before because of the fuss. Ambulance and police folk up and down, flashing lights. Half the neighbours were out asking what was going on. I kept them away. That was the last thing she wanted, explaining to anyone.'

Cathy frowned. 'Odd that no one spotted it before. He'd taken a taxi home that night, I presume? It's too far from town to walk and I believe he was out clubbing.'

'Well, there was a taxi a bit earlier. About half an hour before. It's a cul-de-sac so the lights as they swing around, turning the car, touch the blinds. I said to myself, that'll be number seven home after a boozy night.'

'He went out often, did he?'

'Not often, no, but more than she did, certainly. But why wouldn't they both go out? They were young and had no children.'

Cathy was a little frustrated with the direction the conversation had taken them. The neighbour seemed determined to paint as rosy a picture possible of the couple.

'Was he still conscious when you saw him that night?' she asked rather abruptly.

The man looked surprised. 'He was, yes. Well, barely, to be

fair. He'd been sick. I heard a whole hullaballoo going on. Door opening and shutting and banging about. God, what a noise he'd made. That seemed to quieten down, and I was going to go over and I thought, no, he's come home drunk and she's got him to bed, but I was muddled. The taxi had been earlier. I think he'd stumbled around a fair bit before making it up to the house. I heard her talking. She was in a real state. Shouting at him, trying to get him properly inside. She sounded distressed. That's when I went over to offer my help.'

'I see.'

'Was he able to say what he had taken at that point or...'

'He was past that. Didn't speak at all.'

Cathy smiled. She couldn't hide her disappointment. Nothing the man had said was a surprise. All she had learned was that Michael and Victoria had a rather interfering neighbour to contend with and that Michael's note was vague in the extreme. 'Well, you've been a great help,' she lied. 'It's a shame he wasn't able to tell you anything before he died.'

The man got up. 'I don't suppose... But no, it wasn't really what you were after...'

Cathy froze mid-step.

'There was just one thing,' he said uncertainly. 'Clear went out of my head until you said it like that and it's nothing, really. He was probably just asking us to call the hospital...'

Cathy looked at the man sharply. 'What was it he said?'

'Well, as I say, he didn't talk at all. His face was pale and his lips were sort of twitching. He was trying to tell us something. Well, that's what I thought. She bent down to ask.'

Cathy held her breath.

'He reached out. "H– H– H–," he said. We thought he was trying to say to get him to the hospital, as I say. And I did phone, but there you are. Too late. Perhaps he realised he made a mistake. He'd swallowed whatever it was and regretted it as soon as he saw his wife.' The man looked from Cathy to Chris, clearly delighted to have supplied them with this final piece of information. 'Funny how it went out of my head until now,' he said.

45

'Well, it narrows it down a bit,' Chris said. 'H could stand for Hughie or Huxley. What are the rest of them called?'

'There's just Sara, Jennifer and Ettie. Obviously, Agnes is dead so it could hardly be her and anyway, she starts with an A.'

Chris raised an eyebrow. 'Ettie could be short for Henrietta. Anyone else?'

'There's Saj, obviously, but he's above suspicion and he doesn't start with an H anyway.'

'It might not have been the name of the murderer, even,' Chris said, his hands resting on the steering wheel. 'Maybe the old boy was right. He was saying "hospital," and "get me there damn quick!"'

Cathy sighed.

'Or,' Chris continued, 'maybe he was saying: "help" and rightly so. He knew he was dying and he couldn't do anything to save himself at that point.' He looked at her. 'I'm sorry if you're disappointed. But, what did you expect? His supposed suicide note was hardly going to incriminate anyone, and as for his final words, or rather noises...'

'Okay, Okay,' she said. 'Let's just go.'

He started the car and grinned at her. 'You are a pig-headed thing, aren't you? I'm honoured, in a way, that I was the chosen one. I thought Suzalinna would be backup there once more.'

Cathy chewed a fingernail and didn't answer.

'You two are friends again, aren't you? You're not still angry at her for disappearing without your permission?'

She looked at him reproachfully. 'Don't be ridiculous. Suz is at work. She was delighted to hear about your return from Australia, by the way.'

'Oh, so you told her I was back, did you?'

'Why do you always...?' she began and blushed.

Chris laughed. 'Well, I assume she'll grill me about my intentions towards you sooner or later. No doubt, she'll be furious to hear I was part of the investigation instead of her. Where are we headed, anyway? Home, I assume?'

'The hospital.'

He looked at her sharply, but when she didn't explain he sighed and started the engine.

Chris took them along the high street. They passed the chemist and Cathy saw a patient she knew. The woman raised a hand to acknowledge her. Cathy smiled, and they drove on. They came to a set of temporary traffic lights. Some roadworks were in place.

'I forgot about this bit being closed off. It's the bank,' he said, drumming his fingers on the steering wheel.

Cathy peered ahead and to the left. There was a whole section of the road blocked off with orange and white cones.

'Remember the attempted robbery?'

She shook her head.

The lights were changing, and they couldn't pass. Cathy gazed out as they crawled by.

'What on earth happened?'

The wall of the bank had been damaged, but it was the house next to it that was mainly affected. The bottom two windows were blackened. A line of tape stopped pedestrians from passing too close.

'My burns victim,' Chris said. 'Your receptionist's aunt.'

'The fire. It was an explosion?' She flopped back in her seat. 'Of course.'

Chris shook his head sadly.

They accelerated and the shell of a house was behind them. Soon they were taking the road out of town towards the hospital.

Cathy, who had been twisting her hands in her lap, sighed deeply. She took out her mobile and keyed in a message. She received a reply almost immediately and smiled broadly. Then she settled back more comfortably. Chris glanced across at her. Her face held a look he had not seen before, but anyone who knew her would have said it was undoubtedly an expression of triumph.

46

'I'm sorry to interrupt,' Cathy faltered, her confidence rapidly waning. She looked imploringly at Saj.

'What is this, Cath?' he hissed, coming closer to her.

'It'll only take ten minutes, maximum. I thought the secretaries' office, if no one minds. Please, Saj. I promise it's for a good reason.'

Hughie had just walked through from the back of the lab and saw her. Cathy's heart quickened as he approached.

'Oh yes?' he said as he neared them. 'Klava sent their rep again? I'd not give this troublemaker the time of day, Dr Bhat. She's been sniffing around here before and gave me a false name. I've no idea who she is. Nothing but disruption. I'd not be surprised if she wasn't from the press trying to get an inside story on Michael.'

'She doesn't work for the press or Klava,' Saj answered shortly. 'Hughie, get the girls through here. The professor's in the middle of a post-mortem, Cathy. He can't be disturbed.'

She nodded. 'I suppose it'll have to do.'

Hughie looked furious, but he did as Saj said.

They gathered awkwardly in the office. Sara hastily moved

some of the files from a chair, and Hughie sat beside her. It was the first time Cathy had seen the secretary at work, and she looked awful. Beneath her eyes were two purple shadows. Cathy wondered if she would ever come to terms with Michael's death. The way her gaze seemed to dart around the room, she was constantly looking for him.

Ettie and Jennifer perched on what must have been Agnes's old table. It had been cleared of work and the computer was off. Odd that no one seemed to treat the desk with any reverence. But then Agnes had been less than popular, Cathy was quite sure. They'd need a replacement secretary. Perhaps two, she thought, glancing across at Sara once more as she fidgeted in her seat.

Saj stood by the door next to Cathy. She could tell how uneasy he was without needing to look at him.

'Everyone,' he began, but stopped, not knowing what Cathy wanted from him.

'Thanks, Saj. Look, I'm sorry to interrupt your day like this,' Cathy said. 'I know how busy the labs are and I promise I won't take up any more of your time than I have to. I couldn't leave it any longer. It sounds melodramatic, but I had to explain before more harm was caused. Someone has already died because they knew too much. If anyone else jumped to the same conclusion as Agnes, I suspect that they too might be in the same situation as her. And the person in question is quite prepared, I believe, to kill again.'

There was a stunned silence. Cathy looked at Jennifer and Ettie. The girls stared back, unblinking. But the spell was broken and Jennifer nudged her colleague and smirked.

'Jennifer, we've not been introduced formally. I suspect you'd not find it such a laughing matter if you knew the depths of depravity right here in this hospital. Having murdered two people in cold blood can't have been easy, but now it's been done, I doubt the perpetrator would hesitate in protecting themselves again. That's what desperation does for you.' Cathy turned.

Hughie stared back defiantly. 'What? You can't mean, me?'

'I was concerned about your character from the start, Hughie. You all had a reason to wish Michael ill, but you, above all others, had an axe to grind. You were in very real danger yourself. The black eye? You had become embroiled in something unsavoury. Goodness knows what brought you to that point. Perhaps it began as a bit of matey banter in a bar in town. You worked up at the hospital and maybe you boasted about the hazardous chemicals that you had to deal with daily. This is all conjecture, of course, but your name was passed from one person to another and a meeting arranged. I expect you were short on cash. You always had a chip on your shoulder about the discrepancy in pay between the doctors and technicians. Maybe this was your way of evening it up.'

Hughie laughed, but Cathy knew she was correct.

'You refused to acknowledge where the chemicals were going. I think you were given an order and siphoned off what you could. When things happened in Glainkirk itself, I suspect you could no longer put your head in the sand. You wanted out, but you were already in far too deep. Hence the black eye.' All the while, Hughie had been shaking his head, but Cathy continued, 'And Michael was only making things more complicated by attempting to blackmail you, wasn't he?'

'What?'

She nodded, now warming to her cause. 'There's no point in denying it. He had a hold over you. Who better to have seen what was going on than a lazy junior doctor with time on his hands? Saj?' She turned to her friend. 'The missing chemicals. I realise that the Sodium Azide was of concern but there had been other incidents.'

Saj nodded. 'We thought it was the courier at fault. The company said that they had been sent...'

'This was Klava?' Cathy interrupted.

'You know it was.'

'I looked into the company a good deal, as did Suzalinna. They produce chemicals for laboratory work, preservatives and fixatives, that sort of thing. They also have a sister company involved in the research. They hope to launch a new drug relating to cardiovascular disease.'

'Yes... I don't see...?' Saj looked confused. She had already asked a lot of him in allowing her to speak to the pathology team. She swallowed.

'No, perhaps I should go back a bit,' Cathy conceded. 'I had several concerns about Michael's death from the start. For one, it seemed odd to commit suicide on a work night out. His note worried me as well. Why leave it in his wallet? The alternative, of course, was appalling. Murder. I'll admit, that until Agnes died, I was still willing to go along with the suicide nonsense like the rest of you, simply to keep the peace.'

Saj looked at her desperately.

'But Agnes didn't fall accidentally down the stairs, I'm afraid. Someone pushed her. She knew too much and had already told the killer that she suspected them. Agnes, positioned in this office,' Cathy said, walking across the room and standing so that she faced the door, as Agnes would have done, 'was in the perfect position to watch people coming and going. The window,' she pointed, 'allows the secretaries to see everything that goes on. They watched every single person who came in or out of the department.'

The group turned as she said this, just as Suzalinna, dressed in her A&E scrubs, followed by Chris and Victoria, Michael's widow, walked in.

The room was already very crowded and there was a bit of

confusion as people resettled themselves, but Cathy looked up sharply. Chris met her gaze. They had both heard the soft sound of footsteps retreating just moments before and a hollow cough in the corridor.

'Chris?' she said, a wave of panic rising in her throat.

He only paused a moment, hearing the urgency in her voice.

'The labs, now, Chris! Don't let him get away!'

47

'Professor,' Cathy said as he and Chris came into the room. The old man fumbled with his white coat, trying to put his spectacles into the top pocket.

Hughie got up and offered his chair but Professor Huxley shook his head and stood, arms folded, by the door. Chris hovered just in case he was needed once more.

'What is all this about? Why have we stopped work and who are you?'

'I'm Dr Cathy Moreland. I'm a close friend of Dr Bhat's and I have been looking into the suspicious deaths linked to your pathology department.'

'I beg your pardon?'

'You heard what I said.' Cathy grew angry. 'I find it unbelievable that you will accept Michael's death as a suicide. Perhaps I'm being unfair but you, as clinical lead, should steer the department to safety, not put your head in the sand.'

'I hardly think it's one of my responsibilities. I have enough on my plate without...'

'But you were trying,' Cathy interrupted. 'You knew there was a nasty undercurrent in the labs since Michael had begun working here. People had been bickering. That was why you suggested the meal out that night. The whole thing was your idea, wasn't it?'

The professor spluttered. His face was now a deep red.

'I spoke to Agnes the night she was killed, or rather, murdered,' Cathy added, cruelly. 'She told me that she had overheard you asking the taxi to take you back to the hospital. In the middle of the night, Professor Huxley? It seems too strange. Unless you were coming back for a reason? Michael was, by that point, quite incapable of looking after himself. How easy to pick him up in a taxi after he had fallen out of the club, take him home, and on the way, offer him a drink of water to sober him up? It wasn't right, him going home in a state like that to his wife, was it?'

'I know nothing about it. I didn't put anything in his drink and I know nothing of his wife.'

'This woman lost her husband!' Cathy shouted, turning to point to Victoria, who stood in the corner looking afraid. She hoped Suzalinna had explained what was happening on the way up from ENT with her and Chris. What must the girl be thinking, and to have to be here in the room with these awful people too? But it had to come out. Victoria, of all people, deserved that.

Cathy gently turned to Victoria. 'I am sorry to ask you to come here. I realise it's unpleasant. I'd have spoken to you before now, but I didn't want to offend. I saw your neighbour earlier. He told me about the note.'

Victoria nodded.

She looked so frail and alone standing there. Cathy almost wanted to hug her.

'Yes,' Victoria said. 'But there's something I don't understand. It's been worrying me...'

Cathy nodded. 'About the wallet turning up the day after?

Yes. That troubled me too. The paramedics should have spotted it, or police that night, really. I mean, how could it go unnoticed? Your nosy neighbour told me that, come daylight, he hot-footed it round to your house with an offering of scones. More like an excuse to interfere, if you ask me.'

A smile flashed across Victoria's face, and then she was gaunt and solemn once more.

'He found the wallet with the suicide note in it, lying by your path. I realise this is terrible to hear, Victoria, but it can only mean one thing...'

'The murderer was creeping about outside that night? Oh, it makes me feel horrible.' The young woman shuddered. 'After everyone had left, they came back and dropped the wallet to cover their tracks?'

Cathy looked very grave indeed. 'Not quite,' she said.

The room was completely still. Cathy looked at each expectant face.

'The handwriting concerned me...' she began slowly. 'I assume you were convinced it was Michael's?' she asked Victoria. 'Suzalinna, you put the idea in my head, as it happens. I'm sorry.' Cathy smiled, now forgetting the rest of the department. 'You did all the legwork and here I am, stealing your thunder. But you saw Saj had written in the professor's research folder, that's what made me think. You knew right away it was him, didn't you?'

Suzalinna nodded. 'You know I did, Cath,' she hissed. 'Most women would recognise their husband's handwriting.'

Cathy finally turned to Saj. 'I'm sorry, Saj. Both Suz and I doubted you. And you were above suspicion. Michael didn't think it was you. According to his neighbour, he died with the murderer's name on his lips. He was trying to say something as he died. He reached out to his wife to speak. I stupidly assumed it was Victoria he was talking to, but it wasn't... He was actually talking to his neighbour.'

Everyone waited.

'"H", he said. I assumed it was H for Hughie or Huxley, but it wasn't that at all.' She looked up at Chris, who still stood in the doorway, his broad shoulders blocking any exit. He returned her gaze, but with a quizzical expression. Cathy swallowed. 'He reached out for his wife, soon to be his widow,' she continued, 'and was attempting to say: "her", but rather than reaching out to Victoria, he was pointing...'

There was an agonising moan. It sounded like a wounded animal. She didn't try to run, but instead, collapsed slowly to the floor and covered her face with her hands. It was over.

48

Cathy left it until that evening. The dust had settled by then and emotions weren't running so high. As it turned out, Sara wasn't surprised to see her.

'Oh,' she said simply when she answered the door. 'It's you. I had wondered...'

Cathy stepped into the hallway. 'Your husband?'

'He's at the bottom of the garden.'

Cathy raised her eyebrows.

'My mother's house. The granny flat. He's begun clearing things out. I think it was an excuse, really. I don't blame him. It's been building up gradually. I found some herbal pills stuffed down the side of his bed a few months ago. Something to boost his mood. I suppose I can't have been much fun to live with.'

Cathy nodded. 'If I can help your husband, I will, but for now, I'm glad you're alone. I think you must realise why I've come.'

'You'd better sit down,' Sara said, and gestured to one of the armchairs. 'I wondered if you'd known. You seem to have worked everything else out. I thought it only natural that you'd find that out too.'

'I understand things must have been difficult...'

Sara nodded. 'But it's not a defence, of course. I know I was wrong.'

Cathy nodded, but she remained unconvinced.

They sat for some moments in silence.

'Will you tell the police?' Sara asked.

Cathy sighed. She had been struggling to decide what best to do since the previous day. Attempted murder was an appalling crime after all, even if she had phrased it in her mind as euthanasia.

'If it counts for anything, she actually begged me to end it for her.'

Cathy was suddenly filled with anger. 'She was suffering from dementia. You were meant to be her caregiver, not her killer. How could you know what she might feel the following day? How could you judge how meaningful her life was?' Her hands were shaking and her breathing was short.

'If you'd seen her... She was a shell. She was nothing. If I hadn't been so stupid in taking the wrong stuff, she'd have died quickly. Instead, she lay there for God knows how long to die of "natural causes". What was natural about that?'

Cathy knew it hadn't been a mistake of Sara's making. In fact, Hughie had stolen the real poison long before, leaving her with a box of what might easily have been talcum powder, for all she knew. It was pitiful really. You couldn't make it up. Sara had taken the bottle with her to the restaurant that evening, not planning an attempt to kill Michael, but because she didn't know what else to do with the evidence. Throughout the meal, she must have sat with the thought of her mother dying at home on her conscience and the bottle of what she believed to be poison in her jacket pocket.

'The post-mortem showed nothing,' Sara said defiantly. 'I did no wrong in the end.'

Cathy grimaced. What she said was quite true. 'You'll relinquish your post as secretary in the hospital.'

Sara stammered, but Cathy wouldn't allow her to interrupt. She raised her voice. 'I will not have you working in that place. I will see you at the surgery on a three-monthly basis. This will not be forgotten easily. Please let me warn you that you have escaped formal justice but I will not forget, I doubt your husband will either if he hears.'

When she left, she still felt torn. She knew that Sara didn't regret her actions, and if she had the choice, she'd still do it again. Cathy wondered how the secretary might reflect on things in a couple of days once the realisation of her guilt being known had sunk in. Cathy was convinced that her husband must be fully aware. How would their marriage survive?

As she drove home to change for dinner at Suzalinna's house, she reflected on how she felt about the situation herself. She empathised with Sara and, in truth, she had been involved in decision-making that had contributed to the hastening of a patient's death, as had all doctors. But by virtue of her most fundamental professional commitments, she had sworn never to directly or intentionally cause the end of life. First, do no harm, was what she had pledged when she qualified as a doctor. If anything, she felt more strongly about it now than she had done all those years before.

49

'I'm still confused,' Chris admitted, shaking his head and smiling up at her.

'You've chosen a dud, darling,' Suzalinna teased, and nudged her friend. 'It was me you should have asked for help this morning, not him. I know he thinks he's a clever surgeon now, but really?'

The friends were seated side-by-side on a rattan sofa in Suzalinna's conservatory. Suzalinna had lit the candles on the windowsill and, now that it was dark outside, the room had a warm, flickering glow. Chris, rather than sitting opposite on one of the cushioned chairs, was on the rug at Cathy's feet. Suzalinna had squeezed her friend's arm half a dozen times since they had gathered that evening to dissect the events of the day. She was thrilled that Cathy had found herself a potential partner who she actually approved of.

'It took long enough,' she whispered to Cathy, and winked. Cathy had blushed and rolled her eyes.

'So why did you and Chris go this morning to interrogate the nosy neighbour? You might have waited for me to finish work,' Suzalinna persisted.

'See, I knew you were annoyed,' Cathy said. 'Listen, Suz, and don't take offence, but you can be abrupt...'

Suzalinna looked momentarily outraged and then began to giggle.

'You'd have frightened the life out of the old man.' Cathy laughed and then became serious. 'No, I had to tread carefully there. Most of the evidence rested on his recollection of the evening.'

'What was it that finally made you think it was Victoria?' Saj asked, coming through with a tray of champagne glasses.

'When I heard Agnes had gone to visit her following Michael's death, it rang alarm bells,' Cathy confessed.

'But it was just a token bereavement visit from the department,' Saj said. 'It could have been anyone visiting with the flowers. Agnes just happened to offer.'

'Really? I don't think so, Saj. Agnes was a smart woman and rather spiteful. She knew a whole lot about the pathology lab and the people in it. She could easily see what was going on from her vantage point in the office. One evening, she saw Victoria come in. It was after most of the department had left for the day. That was when Victoria stole a small amount of Sodium Azide. The bottle was fully visible in the fume cupboard with hazard-warning signs all over it. She had a universal container ready with her, and she was quick. The fact that Hughie pocketed the rest of the stuff later was entirely down to chance and it helped muddy the waters a good deal. It was ideal, really. Victoria could have used anything to kill Michael, but it needed to be traceable back to the lab in case the suicide note didn't work. That was a rushed afterthought. She panicked with the police questions and thought it would stop any further investigation. She was right. The police fell for it.'

'But why?' Chris asked. 'Why did she kill him at all?'

Cathy sighed. 'I feel rather sorry for Victoria, in a way. Of course, she did a terrible thing, and killing Agnes was inexcusable, but life married to Michael was surely pretty awful. Every day, he must have made it torture for her with his infidelities.'

'Not the other secretary, Sara?' Suzalinna asked.

'No, but Ettie and he had been carrying on. I think the over-flirtatious banter with Sara was a horrible ironic joke between the pair of them. Sara must have suffered at their hands, but imagine how much worse it was for Michael's long-suffering wife. You know what the hospital's like. Gossip goes around like wildfire. You heard about my bipolar fast enough,' she said to Chris and smiled. 'Anyway, the affair got back to Victoria, and I suspect she accused him. That would have added to the fun for Michael though.'

'So, at the meal, it wasn't Victoria he phoned from outside?' Suzalinna asked.

'No, it was Ettie, believe it or not. The pair of them were having a whale of a time laughing at the others behind their backs that night. Ettie was through in the toilets, talking to him on her mobile after Jennifer and Sara had just left. It was horrible, really.'

'So, Victoria stole the chemical from our lab?' Saj repeated, still trying to piece the sequence of events together.

'I think you told me yourself that wives do sometimes come to visit their husbands when I suggested that Suzalinna had been there without your knowledge? Did you see Victoria there, Saj? I did wonder.'

'Oh goodness, now you say it, yes, I did, but it went out of my head.'

'You make the most appalling witness, Saj,' Suzalinna scolded. 'Thank God, Cathy has eagle eyes.'

Cathy smiled at her friends and was relieved to see Saj looking affectionately at his wife.

'Victoria knew about the work night out and that was when she decided to do it. She waited up for him to come home. His neighbour admitted that it was a bit odd. He heard Michael's taxi dropping him off a good ten minutes before Victoria started calling out. He assumed he had made a mistake, or that Michael had been stumbling around in the dark all that time. Victoria made a big show of things on the doorstep, calling out and trying to get him inside. In fact, he had already been inside the house and poisoned. She was dragging him into the hallway to make it look like he'd just arrived.'

'My God!' Suzalinna said with satisfaction. 'You are clever, Cath.'

'Well, so are you,' Cathy said, not wanting to take all the credit. 'You worked out what was going on with the professor, after all.'

'Eventually,' Suzalinna conceded.

'Yes, you did take a while.'

Saj looked uncomfortable.

'Is he going to retire then, Saj?' Cathy asked.

'How did you know?'

'I couldn't believe either of you were involved in manipulating the data for his cardiovascular research project. I looked through the folder and the project had been running for a long time. There were so many places where you had asterisked mistakes and rewritten the correct findings. It got to the point that you added an extra line to the table to account for his errors. His is vascular, I assume, hence the urgency to do the study?'

Saj nodded. 'Yes, he has vascular dementia. His consultant diagnosed him last year and he got it into his head that doing this final project for Klava would be his parting gift to the medical world before he retired. It wasn't for his own ends that he did the research. He knew he was beyond any medical help. It was painful to watch him deteriorate, albeit slowly. I suppose he was going back to the labs in the evening. Maybe even confusing night and day, desperate to stay at his beloved work as long as he could.'

'No!' Chris exclaimed. 'When I ran after him today, I had no idea.'

'I was afraid, after hearing us talk, he might do something silly,' Cathy admitted. 'The labs are full of dangerous chemicals, as we all know.'

'He's not the suicidal type,' Saj said. 'And he's fine now. I drove him home this evening, and we had a long talk. His wife and I have been discussing it from time to time. I wanted to have her support when I suggested he step down. He's been okay to work with my supervision until now. But he handed in his resignation to the health board this afternoon. I thought he'd be devastated, but he looked relieved in the end.'

'So, you'll be another member of staff down?' Suzalinna asked.

'More than one,' Cathy corrected. 'Don't forget Hughie.'

Suzalinna sighed. 'Yes, Hughie has fallen from grace rather spectacularly.'

'I missed that bit,' Chris said. 'I arrived too late.'

'The bank, remember? We drove past earlier,' Cathy explained. 'I don't think Hughie knew where the stolen chemicals were going, but he got paid handsomely to supply them. He had been asked for something flammable and potentially volatile this time. That's where the Sodium Azide came in. I read that it was used in airbags so it was ideal as an explosive...'

'For the ATM? They tried to blow it off the wall to steal money but instead set fire to the house next door? My poor patient was trapped inside.' Chris looked aghast.

Cathy nodded. 'Hughie will have some serious explaining to do.'

'And what about your patient, Cathy?' Suzalinna asked.

'Who do you mean?'

Suzalinna put her glass down on the table next to her. 'Sara Wiseman. What about her? You thought she was caught up in things at the start, didn't you?'

Cathy looked thoughtful. 'She won't be returning to the pathology labs, that's for sure.'

'Well,' Chris said, 'and I thought Glainkirk would be a bit dull after Australia too.' He raised his glass. 'I propose a toast.'

Saj and Suzalinna smiled and raised their glasses. Cathy hurriedly joined them.

'To renewed friendships?' Chris asked.

'Well, I'm hoping it's going to be a bloody sight more than that!' Suzalinna countered.

But Cathy hadn't noticed. Chris was smiling at her, and the rest of the room had all but disappeared. 'I'll drink to that,' she said. 'Cheers.'

THE END

ACKNOWLEDGEMENTS

To my editor, Clare and the rest of the Bloodhound team, thank you as always for keeping me on schedule and making the process fun. Many thanks to my mother and father for the support. My greatest thanks go to my husband and son for their unerring love and the endless supply of cups of tea, biscuits and banana milkshakes to get me through the first draft! Perhaps most importantly, thank you to all of the readers who continue to read along and enjoy the Dr Cathy Moreland Mysteries. Your encouragement really keeps me going and I can't wait to share the next book in the series with you!

A NOTE FROM THE PUBLISHER

Thank you for reading this book. If you enjoyed it please do consider leaving a review on Amazon to help others find it too.

We hate typos. All of our books have been rigorously edited and proofread, but sometimes mistakes do slip through. If you have spotted a typo, please do let us know and we can get it amended within hours.

info@bloodhoundbooks.com